Holiday Hijinks

Samantha Baca

Cover Design: Richard Baca
Image(s): DepositPhotos

Contents

<u>One</u>
Holly

"It's so beautiful up here," I said dreamily as I pressed my nose against the window to get a better look at the snow-covered forest surrounding us. "It's going to be such a romantic weekend."

I glanced over my shoulder at Henry, batting my eyes at him playfully, but his attention was laser-focused on the road in front of us, so he hadn't noticed.

Not that it was odd for him. He was always so uptight about everything; I rarely saw him relaxed and enjoying himself these days. I knew that he must be stressed with putting together such an elaborate plan to finally pop the question to me after five long years, so I was cutting him some slack—even if it felt like he was pulling further away by the day.

I was a city girl—born and raised—and rarely took the time to go on adventures in the mountains. When Henry suggested that we come up to his family's cabin for the weekend, I couldn't say no. I'd even gone to great lengths to google what one should pack for a *wilderness retreat*. It was disappointing when I got a handful of results leading me to sites full of flannel and long johns. How the hell was I supposed to make *that* look sexy?

"It's going to be cold," he replied, ignoring my comment about it being a romantic weekend.

Okay, okay, I like the secrecy bit. I'll just continue to pretend like I don't know he's going to ask me to marry him and make me the happiest—and richest—woman alive!

"Yeah, but the cabin has a heater, so we'll be fine."

I lifted my shoulders and let them fall. The loose neck of the ivory cowl neck sweater I was wearing slid to the side, exposing my shoulder. I had picked this one to wear on our drive out, along with my skinny jeans tucked neatly into the sexy knee-high boots I bought at the last minute. Henry shook his head when he saw my outfit, and I knew he must've been frustrated to have to wait that long before ripping it off of me.

When he didn't answer, I felt a slight tingle of dread creep down my spine.

"There is a heater, right?" I asked, turning to face him.

He glanced briefly at me before turning his attention back to the road.

"There's a fireplace."

My eyebrows shot up.

"And a heater. RIGHT?"

He rubbed his lips together the way he always did when he didn't want to tell me something.

"Henry Aaron Smith—you're taking me to a secluded cabin in the middle of the woods, and it doesn't even have a heater?!"

"I told you that it was a little *outdated*."

"Yeah, and I thought maybe that meant that your mom had some hideous curtains hung from the seventies or beat-up wood floors. You never said anything about there not being proper heat in the damn place." I turned and folded my arms over my chest, more frustrated with myself for not asking more questions before packing for this damn trip.

"You'll be fine, Holly. My dad grew up in this cabin. His parents did before that. It's not as bad as you're making it sound."

His tone was snappy, as if he was angry with me.

"Why haven't you guys fixed it up? I mean, you have the money to…"

I felt rude for asking, but it wasn't like Henry didn't constantly remind people of his family's empire and the wealth he'd been born into. I didn't know many of the details of how they came to be so well off, but I knew it had something to do with his grandparents, Texas, and a lot of oil. Like A LOT of oil.

"Why fix something that's not broken?" His hand gripped the steering wheel tighter as he slowly turned down another dirt road.

We were literally in the middle of nowhere with snowbanks at least ten feet tall on either side of the SUV. Even if I wanted to turn and run back to the city, I couldn't. I was officially stuck here with him—in a heatless cabin—until Monday.

We kept driving until the road curved, and he stopped in front of a log-looking cabin. He frowned when he noticed the other car parked in front of the garage.

"What's wrong?" I asked.

"My parents are here."

"What?" My head whipped around in panic, looking for them. "Did you invite them?"

He shook his head and grabbed his cell phone from the cupholder in the middle console.

"No, Holly, I didn't invite them. Apparently, they had the same idea as us."

I swallowed hard, nervous about seeing his parents. I'd met them a few times, but they never seemed to like me. We lived in Los Angeles, while they had a massive mansion in Beverly Hills. Needless to say, the holidays were usually spent with them at their house because they didn't like to *slum it* at mine. They never said that, but they didn't have to. Margaret, Henry's mom, had no problem wearing her emotions on her face, which usually gave way to what she was thinking.

"We better get inside before we freeze to death out here," Henry said sternly, climbing out before giving me a chance to process his words.

<u>Two</u>
Holly

We walked through the door, and I felt my stomach knot harder. His parents weren't in the living room, so Henry called out to let them know we were there. The last thing any of us needed right now was surprises that could traumatize us.

I lingered by the door, wrapping my arms around myself to try to get warm. It was freaking cold in here, and they hadn't even bothered to start a fire yet. Maybe they hadn't been there that long, or perhaps they didn't get as cold as I did.

I looked around, taking in the floor-to-ceiling windows that spanned around the small living room. Two leather couches sat in the middle, facing the TV mounted above the fireplace that wasn't lit. Was I bitter about it? Maybe.

Part of me wanted to take a tour through the rest of the cabin, but I stayed put until I knew where Margaret and Stan were. Henry was already looking for them, so I didn't need to.

I was busy browsing through the collection of books lining the bookshelf that was part of the entertainment center when Henry walked in with his parents in tow behind him.

"Mom, dad, you remember Holly," he said, though it sounded a bit forced. He raked a hand through his hair and forced a smile.

"Yes," Margaret said coldly, giving me a judgmental once over before turning to her husband. "Stan, why don't you and Henry go unload the vehicles? It's obvious none of us are getting back down the mountain before this storm hits, so we'll all have to figure out how to share this space *together*." She looked down her nose at me.

"I can help," I volunteered to Henry, not wanting to be left alone with his mom.

I knew that if he were going to propose, he probably wouldn't do so now with them hovering around us. It was a small cabin which meant we were all going to be on top of each other for the next few days.

"In those boots?" His mother rolled her eyes in Stan's direction, not bothering to hide it from me. "You'll fall and break your leg before you even get one bag out of the car. It's fine; I'll help them. You can just stay inside, where it's safe."

I felt my cheeks flame with embarrassment. At least the heat spreading through my body worked to warm me up for a few minutes before it passed.

The three of them went to the car and started unpacking. I was curious why they hadn't just pulled into the garage, where it was dry and not covered with snow, but what did I know? I was just a silly girl from the city who knew nothing about the wilderness.

It was over seven hours to drive to Hope Valley from Los Angeles, and now I was ready to pack up and head home. This was not how I wanted to spend the weekend—cooped up with people who couldn't stand me and a boyfriend who seemed more preoccupied with something he wouldn't talk to me about. I could be enjoying the weather in LA or working on getting new auditions. Lord knew I needed some if I was ever going to achieve my dream of being a movie star.

A few minutes later, the front door flew open, gaining speed as a gust of wind whipped past. Henry pushed inside, setting our luggage behind the couch before helping his mother. Her perfectly manicured nails struggled to keep hold of the bags in her hands before he grabbed them and relieved her of them.

Stan came in right as Henry slipped back outside to grab the rest. Aside from our suitcases, I had a few duffle bags that contained my makeup and bathroom stuff, and Henry had brought a few boxes full of groceries. I had offered to help, but he declined and said he would get things that would last—whatever that meant.

"Um, what room would you like us to take?" I asked as nicely as possible while Margaret lifted the handle to their hard-shell luggage and started pulling.

"Well, we haven't talked about that. We hadn't expected any guests, so I was planning to use the other bedroom for my craft stuff. I guess you guys can take the other room. It's through the kitchen."

She turned on her heel and took off down the hallway.

I muffled the groan that wanted to escape my lips and grabbed my luggage. There were only two doors in the kitchen, so I tried the first one, which ended up being a rather decently stocked pantry of canned goods and gallons of bottled water that lined the floor. I closed it and then opened the other door, gasping when I saw the *room* she was talking about.

It wasn't a room at all. It was the garage that someone had once started to convert to a bedroom but never finished. There were no windows, so I fumbled around, trying to find the light switch when I slipped off the step down that I hadn't seen.

My hands flew in the air as I landed hard on my ass. I let out a slew of curse words as my ass ached from the fall. There was no padding beneath me, just hard concrete.

I bit the inside of my cheek to keep from crying, but it didn't help. The pain was intense and radiated throughout my body. I took a deep, steadying breath and tried to stand up, only to realize that the heel of my boot had broken off in the process.

That was the final straw that broke the camel's back.

I let my head fall forward and covered my face with my hands as the tears started streaming down my face.

"What's wrong?" Henry asked, coming up behind me. He reached in and flicked on the lights.

I held the broken piece of my shoe in the air and kept crying.

"Yeah, well, I could have told you those were the wrong shoes to wear out here," he said before brushing past me and setting the rest of our luggage beside a rickety-looking futon.

I couldn't stop crying to tell him about the fall. It wasn't even just that; it was a combination of things that kept building. The way his mother acted toward me. The fact that his father hadn't said a single word to me. The way Henry had been the entire drive up. The crappy room we would be spending the next few days in when he'd promised me a romantic getaway at his family's cabin. Okay, so maybe he hadn't promised me any romance, but he also didn't forewarn me about what a shitshow this would be.

"The futon is kinda old, so we can decide who's going to sleep on it and who wants to take the couch," he offered, completely dismissing the fact that I was still sitting there crying. He finally looked down at me and then pointed to a small couch in the corner of the room that looked like it had seen better days.

I took one look at it and then cried harder.

"I don't know what you expected, Holly. It's not like we were planning a stay at some fancy resort or something."

I threw my hands in the air and let out a whoosh of air.

"I don't know what I expected either, *Henry*. You've been so distant and aloof with me that I have no idea what's going on. Don't sit there and act like I'm some princess who's throwing a fit about not staying in a five-star establishment. I was fine coming to the cabin with you. In fact, I was excited about it! But now that we're here—with *your parents*—I'm not feeling anything but irritated with how everyone is treating me!"

I knew that I was yelling and his parents could probably hear me, but I didn't care.

It was like something snapped inside him, and the grumpy Henry left.

"I'm sorry," he said softly, coming over and wrapping his arms around me. "I've been super stressed out with stuff at work this week, and it just caught up to me. I was hoping that this weekend would be the break that I needed to reset before the holidays. I didn't mean for it to start off this way, and I honestly had no idea that my parents would be here. Usually, they go to the ranch in Texas and spend the holidays there. I know that it sucks having to sleep in here, but we can try to make the best of it. If not, I can rearrange the living room, and we can sleep up there. It'll be much warmer since we can keep the fire going at night."

The corners of my lips turned up into a smile as I allowed my body to melt against his.

"That sounds like a plan, but what happens when I want to take advantage of you? We can't do *that* in the living room," I whispered playfully.

"No, we can't," he laughed. "But we can come in here for quickies, then go back to the living room."

"Deal," I giggled as he tickled my sides.

His hands slowly caressed my back and then dipped lower, hovering right above my ass when I winced in pain.

"What's wrong?" His eyebrows pulled together in concern.

"I fell and landed on my ass. That's how my heel broke." I held up the piece again to show him.

"Ouch, are you okay?"

"It hurts pretty bad. Definitely going to have a bruise."

"Let me see."

"What?" I pulled back and laughed at him. "I'm not going to show you my ass."

"Why not? I see it every time we have sex."

"Yeah, but that's different." I felt the blush creeping up my neck under the thickness of the sweater.

"You're so weird," he laughed but didn't push further. He

let go and walked back to our luggage, opening his suitcase and pulling out the hoodie on top.

"So, how many bathrooms are there?" I asked, chewing my bottom lip as I prayed that he would say at least two.

"Just one."

I frowned. That sucked. I really wanted to soak in a long, hot bath, but I couldn't easily tie up the only bathroom for a few hours. That wouldn't be fair.

"I'm going to go see what my parents need help with and get the groceries unpacked."

He walked out and left me standing there, *nice Henry* gone just as quickly as he appeared.

<u>Three</u>
Holly

The fire crackled and roared as I curled up on the couch, tucking my feet beneath me. There was no need to wear shoes, but it was still too cold to go without socks. Now I understood why so many of those websites had thick, non-slip socks for sale. Easy to keep you warm without the risk of slipping and falling on hardwood floors because very few cabins would have carpet, given how much snow people would trek in from outside. Not that they had gone into that much detail, but Margaret had when she lectured me about the boots I had been wearing earlier.

We were all holed up in the small space in the living room, with Henry and me sharing the small loveseat while Margaret and Stan spread out on the oversized couch that had recliners. I already knew where I was sleeping tonight.

The conversation had been dull and pretty much one-sided at that. The sun was starting to set, casting a warm reddish-orange glow on the trees outside. My stomach growled, reminding me I hadn't eaten since the breakfast burrito I bought this morning.

"I'm going to go make dinner," I announced, getting up and not bothering to wait for anyone to object.

I wasn't a terrible cook, but I wasn't an award-winning chef, either.

When Henry and I first started dating, he did most of the cooking, and I simply enjoyed it. I was barely eighteen and had just moved out of my parent's house, while he was twenty-three and had just graduated from college. We were as different as different could be, but that was what I always thought pulled us together. You know, opposites attract and all that.

After three months of dating, Henry asked me to move in with him. It was definitely quicker than I had imagined us moving, but I was also in between roommates and needed to find more stable housing. Living with Henry was easy, and he turned out to be one of the best roommates I'd had. Everything since then seemed to fall naturally in place until recently.

I rummaged through the fridge, looking for something to cook but unsure of what Henry had brought and what was his parents. Deciding that I would use this weekend to get in his parents' good graces, I wanted to make dinner for all of us. I was going to be their future daughter-in-law, so it wouldn't hurt to start trying to impress them now.

I preheated the oven and then began prepping the ingredients. It was a dish I'd made for Henry plenty of times, and if he liked it, surely his parents would too. Granted, it was no filet mignon, but it wasn't inedible either. Whether or not I could ever live up to their expectations was still beyond me.

The oven beeped, letting me know it was ready. I slid the foil-covered casserole dish in and closed the door. There wasn't much else that needed to be done, but I still wasn't ready to go back into the living room and sit with them. It was awkward, and I had difficulty getting comfortable on the couch without room to spread out. Not only that, but I had to sit in a way that put a lot of pressure on my hips and ass, which were still sore.

Suddenly remembering I had brought wine, I headed into the garage and rummaged through my bags until I found the bottles I had packed. There were a few that I thought Henry and I would drink with dinner, a few that were planned for our romantic late-night lovemaking, and a bottle of champagne that I added, just in case Henry forgot to bring one to celebrate our engagement with.

I loaded my arms with the bottles and then made my way back into the kitchen.

No one had bothered to ask if they could help with anything, which honestly didn't upset me. I preferred solitude right now, anyway.

I took the liberty of putting the bottles in the fridge to let them chill while I set the table for dinner.

I knew that it shouldn't matter to me that much whether his parents liked me or not, but I literally had nothing else to do with my time than try to get them to. Leisurely, I looked around the kitchen, gathering the things that I needed. I wiped down the table and then found a pile of linens in the pantry that were tucked inside a box.

Choosing to make dinner more to their liking, I grabbed a deep maroon-colored tablecloth and then draped a lace table runner on top of it. It was an odd shape that was narrow at one end and flared out at the other, but I tucked in it and made it work the best I could.

Then I grabbed some wine glasses from the cabinet, as well as some glasses for ice water, and washed the dust off of them. There weren't many dishes to choose from, so I picked the solid white set since it looked less breakable than the fine China sitting next to it.

Once the table was set, I grabbed the loaf of French bread I found on the counter and began cutting it. Dinner already smelled amazing and I couldn't wait to sit down and eat.

I debated which wine to open for dinner but decided to go with a pinot grigio since it would pair well with the chicken. I filled a glass for each person and then went to the freezer to get ice for the water. I frowned when I pushed the button and nothing came out. I opened the door and peeked inside, looking to see if I could find an ice bin instead.

The bin was empty, and I realized that the water line probably wasn't set up for it. I found a small bag of ice cubes and hoped they would work. Once the glasses had enough ice, I grabbed one of the gallon jugs of water out of the pantry and filled them.

I stepped back, impressed with the beautiful display, given there were limited supplies.

The timer on the oven dinged, so I grabbed some potholders and pulled the casserole out, setting it on a trivet in the middle of the table. Next to it, I set down the cutting board with the French bread and a bottle of balsamic oil.

My nerves were at an all-time high as sweat dotted my forehead.

"Dinner's ready," I announced as I walked into the living room and held my hands in front of me.

Stan faked enthusiasm as he plastered on a smile and stood up while Margaret didn't bother to try. She followed her husband into the kitchen, leaving me alone with Henry for a few seconds before we joined them.

"It smells delicious," he whispered, walking behind me as he led me in with his hands on my shoulders.

"They're going to hate it," I muttered right before we went through the door.

HOLIDAY HIJINKS

<u>Four</u>
Holly

"This is…. Lovely." Margaret stared at the display in front of her, not bothering to serve herself.

"Thank you," I said nervously and took my seat. "It's this chicken and rice casserole that Henry loves." I reached over and squeezed his hand, hoping he would jump in and talk it up.

"Chicken?" his mother asked, her eyebrow attempting to lift but permanently frozen in place from the constant supply of Botox.

I nodded slowly, unsure of what the problem was.

She gave me a cold smile and looked at Henry with a look that only a mother could give their child. It was the *what the hell were you thinking* look that my own mother had given me several times in my life.

Henry winced and closed his eyes.

"My mom is a vegetarian."

My eyes widened in horror as I stared at the dish. Not only had I shredded the chicken and spread it throughout, but I also cooked it in chicken broth and then used cream of chicken soup for the casserole mixture.

"I'm so sorry, I didn't know."

She lifted her glass of wine and lifted it to her lips.

"It's fine. Just as I'm sure you didn't know that Stan is twenty-seven years sober and doesn't drink."

I felt my heart sink and looked at the glass of wine in front of him.

"Don't worry, dear; I'll relieve you of that. It looks like I'll be drinking my calories tonight instead." Margaret reached over, took the glass from him, and then set it in front of her as she took another large drink from hers.

"I really am sorry," I apologized, looking between them. "I had no idea."

I turned my attention back to Margaret, feeling bad that I'd ruined dinner, and now she had nothing to eat unless she cooked something herself.

"There's bread if you want to start with that. I can check to see what else there is and make you something," I offered.

"I don't eat bread," she spat out as if I had somehow insulted her—which I probably did.

Henry said nothing as he served himself and then passed the dish to his father. Both of them took heaping portions while his mom sat there drinking her wine and staring at the tablecloth.

"Where did you get all of this?" she asked, pointing to the table runner.

"Oh, I, um, found it in a box in the pantry with a few other linens. I hope you don't mind."

I was in the middle of dishing some of the casserole out onto my plate when she spoke.

"Absolutely I mind," she scoffed, reaching out to run her fingers over the delicate lace fabric. "This isn't a table runner; it was my mother's wedding veil."

The metal serving spoon slipped out of my hand, dropping the chicken casserole onto my plate and sending a spatter of food onto the wedding veil.

"I had no idea," I whispered, covering my mouth with my hand. This was turning into a total and utter disaster.

"Here, I can take it off real quick," I offered, standing up and bumping my glass of wine. I watched in horror as it tipped to the side before Henry's hand reached out and grabbed it.

"Oh, for the love of God, I've had enough." Margaret grabbed both glasses of wine and pushed away from the table before leaving the kitchen.

I covered my face with my hands in embarrassment while the guys continued eating as if nothing had happened. My world was ending before me, and they were stuffing their faces.

I heard a chair scraping against the floor and opened my eyes. Stan's plate still had food, but his water glass was empty. I knew he was heading to the sink to refill it, so I stood up to stop him.

"Here, let me refill that for you," I offered, trying my best to smile despite everything that had happened.

With curious eyes, he handed me his glass and watched as I slid past Henry to open the fridge. I grabbed the gallon of water and started to refill it when I heard a quiet gasp escape Henry's lips.

I spun around and looked between them, trying to figure

out what I had done wrong now.

"Where did you get that?" Henry asked quietly.

The words were stuck in my throat, so I pointed behind them to the pantry.

Henry set his fork down, closed his eyes, and took a deep breath.

"What?" I asked worriedly. "What did I do wrong this time?"

"That's our emergency stash. When the weather gets terrible, it can be hard to get into town for supplies," Stan explained.

"Of course," I sighed and handed him the glass of emergency water. "I'm so sorry. Again, I didn't know."

He pulled his lips into a thin line that was supposed to be a smile but wasn't. After that, we all ate in silence. Henry insisted that he would handle the dishes, which was probably the best idea at this point.

Deciding that I couldn't face his parents right now, I retreated to the cold garage and added a few more layers of clothing to keep from losing a limb to frostbite.

It was going to be a long weekend.

Five
Holly

"Are you going to hide in here all night?" Henry asked, leaning against the doorframe but not bothering to come into the freezing cold garage.

I wrapped my arms tighter around myself and felt my teeth chattering.

"It's not like anyone misses me," I snorted and rolled my eyes.

"That's not true. I do."

I pinned him with a look that called him on his bullshit.

He crossed the room and sat down on the futon beside me.

"I'm sorry that today was so rough and eventful. I should have been in the kitchen helping you make dinner. I just didn't trust my parents not to come in and harass you while you were cooking, so I thought I was keeping the calm by keeping them out of your way. I let you down so much today, and I hate that."

"It's okay," I said softly as he reached over and pulled me closer to him.

I yelped in pain, and he immediately let go and looked down at my ass.

"You should go soak in a hot bath," he offered, his eyes softening as he looked up at me.

"Thanks, but I don't think so," I laughed. "There's no way I'm tying up the only bathroom for a few hours. I'll *never* live that down, along with everything else that happened today."

"Don't be so hard on yourself; they were honest mistakes."

"I'm sure your parents don't think so. I tried to feed your mom meat, gave your dad alcohol, and dropped chicken casserole on your grandmother's wedding veil. Why was that in the pantry anyway?"

He tilted his head back and laughed.

"I have no idea. But I'll go talk to them and let them know you're going to soak for a bit. Grab some of your bath stuff, and I'll meet you in the bathroom."

I was reluctant to take him up on the offer, but the way my body was aching, I didn't have much of a choice.

He headed back inside while I rummaged through my duffle bags and collected the items I wanted.

When I found him in the living room, he was talking to his parents, who got up the moment they saw me. They walked past without saying a word and closed their bedroom door.

"They're going to retire to their room early tonight," he explained though I could read the words he didn't say all over his face. *They hate you. They wish you weren't here. You're inconveniencing them.*

"Okay," I whispered, feeling my throat tighten with emotion.

"Let me show you how to work the tub."

I was going to object and tell him that I knew how to use one, but when I followed him into the bathroom, I realized that this wasn't an ordinary bathtub. It was a large soaking one with jets and different settings with an LED touch-screen to control them.

He turned on the water and explained the different features, but all I could think about at that moment was how badly I had to pee. I had gotten so caught up with everything earlier that I didn't realize I hadn't gone since the gas station we stopped at right before we got to the cabin.

I squeezed my thighs together and squirmed, hoping he would leave me alone so I could pee. As if sensing my discomfort, he glanced at me doing the potty dance and nodded.

"Just call me if you need help with the settings. I've already programmed it with what I think you'll like, but I can come back if you want to change anything."

"Okay, thanks."

Once he was gone, I closed the door and locked it before rushing to the toilet.

After what felt like the longest pee in the world, I dipped my hand into the running water to test the temperature. Henry had set it perfectly where it was hot enough to melt my troubles away but not hot enough to burn me.

I opened the bag of coconut Epsom salts, sprinkled some in, and then set out the loofah and bottle of body wash I had just bought for the trip. There were towels hanging by the tub, but I didn't trust that they weren't special or reserved for the Queen or something, so I opened the large cabinets on the far end of the wall and grabbed a basic-looking towel from the pile. Odds were it was a safe bet if it was mixed with the others.

Slowly I climbed into the oversized tub and sank into the water, closing my eyes as it warmed the chill I hadn't been able to shake since we got here.

I grabbed my phone and turned on one of the audiobooks I had been listening to while resting my head against the pillow Henry had set up for me. The water felt amazing and was just what the doctor ordered.

I didn't know how long I had my eyes closed, but suddenly, the room was silent as my audiobook ended. I swiped my finger and checked the text notifications that had come in from Henry. Usually, I heard them, but I must have been so relaxed and out of it that I completely missed them. I checked the time and noticed they were sent half an hour ago.

Henry: Hey, how much longer do you think you'll be? My mom needs to use the restroom.

Henry: Sorry, I don't want to rush you, but my mom really needs to go. I told them to go before you got in, but they didn't listen for whatever reason.

Henry: Don't worry about it. She went outside. Enjoy your bath.

I read the last one again and cringed. Not only had I cooked a meal she couldn't eat, but I also used mother's veil as a table runner, and now I'd forced her to pop a squat in the woods. This wasn't going to be good.

Trying to move as quickly as possible, I grabbed the towel and wrapped it around my body before stepping out of the tub. I looked down for a plug to pull and couldn't find anything. Then I looked at the control panel and assumed it was on there, but now wasn't the time to break their fancy tub by button mashing. I'd just leave it for Henry to take care of so I didn't screw anything else up.

I looked around for the pajamas I'd picked out but frowned when I remembered that I had left them on the futon. Not having any other options, I quickly put on the clothes I was wearing earlier and hung the towel on the rack mounted to the back of the door.

I hoped to sneak out without running into his parents, but luck didn't seem to be in my favor today. As soon as I opened the door, his mother came out of their room and glared at me.

My mouth opened to say something but snapped shut when I realized I didn't know what to say.

Henry came around the corner at that moment and seemed startled to see me.

"Hey, I was just coming to check on you," he said happily, avoiding the look his mom was giving him.

"Sorry, I didn't hear my phone and lost track of time."

"No worries, it's fine. I'm going to use the restroom real quick."

"Oh, do you mind draining the tub? I wasn't sure how to do it and didn't want to break something," I said quietly, tucking my chin to my chest.

"Sure, I'll take care of it. I'll be done in a few minutes, mom."

"Don't rush on my account. I'll be waiting for the hot water to return."

She turned on her heel and shut the bedroom door on us.

Henry tried to smile, but neither of us felt it. I left him to his business and went to the garage to take care of mine.

Just as I expected, the pajamas I picked earlier were still sitting on top of my suitcase. I felt silly now for wearing them, but when I packed, I had expected it to be just Henry and me. I also thought I would be happily engaged by now, so I didn't bother to pack warm or comfy—I packed sexy.

I picked up the black lace lingerie and matching robe and held it up. There was absolutely no way I was going to wear that. I hadn't even paid attention to it when I pulled it out earlier; I was just too excited about the bath that I didn't think about anything else.

I opened my suitcase and looked around for something decent to wear. His parents had already deemed me to be incompetent, and the last thing I wanted was to prove them right.

There weren't many options, given it was a short weekend trip. I had a few pairs of jeans, some bulky sweaters, a couple of tank tops to wear underneath them, and then sexy lingerie. It wasn't going to be comfortable sleeping in jeans, but then again, it would be much less comfortable if his parents spotted me in the crotchless underwear I brought to seduce their son.

I sighed and got dressed, tucking the lingerie into the bottom of the suitcase, so I didn't accidentally pull it out again.

Henry was sitting on the larger couch when I went to the living room. I looked around for his parents, but they were nowhere to be found. Thankfully.

He patted the spot beside him, so I gently sat down, making

sure not to put too much pressure on my swollen backside.

"Did the bath help any?" he asked, brushing a strand of blonde hair from my face.

"It did," I smiled. "But I feel terrible for taking so long in there. I completely lost track of time."

He kissed my forehead, then looked back at the TV and flipped through the channels with the remote in his other hand.

"Don't worry about it. It's not a big deal."

"Tell that to your mother," I bit out sarcastically. "She had to pee in the woods, and then I used all the hot water."

"It comes with the territory. She knows that."

"Yeah, but if I weren't here, she wouldn't have to worry about either."

He didn't respond, which was probably for the better. The last thing I wanted to do was keep obsessing over how much Margaret didn't like me.

We watched some sports channel for a bit until Henry yawned and lifted his arm from around my shoulders.

"I think I'm going to call it a night," he announced.

"Okay." I started to get up but stopped when he frowned at me.

"What are you doing?" he asked.

"Getting up so you can go to bed."

I looked at the couch I was sitting on, wondering if he had changed his mind about sleeping in there. I really, really hoped he didn't. I couldn't stand the thought of sleeping on the hard futon in the freezing-cold garage.

"You're fine," he laughed. "I'll sleep on the other couch."

"But it's way too small. You won't fit comfortably. I can take that one, and you can sleep on this one."

He walked over to the other couch, removed the cushions, and then pulled a cloth handle that released a pull-out bed. It was small and definitely wouldn't fit both of us, but it was decent-sized for him.

"Oh," I laughed. "I didn't expect that to be in there."

"I used to sleep on this couch a lot as a kid. It's pretty comfy, actually."

I smiled and looked at the couch I was sitting on, wondering what the most comfortable position would be. I figured we could both use one of the recliners and sleep there, but now that I had the entire couch to myself, it looked comfier to lie across it.

 Henry grabbed us some blankets and found a pillow for me to use. I knew that once he was ready for bed, that was it. So, I said goodnight to him, then got situated on the couch with one of the books I'd decided to try from the bookshelf. There were a lot of non-fiction ones about success and building your empire, but there were also a few older romance-looking ones tucked into the corner.

The fire put out a surprising amount of heat but started to die down right before I fell asleep. Not wanting us to get cold, I grabbed a few logs from the wooden basket next to the fireplace and tossed them in, just as I had seen Henry do earlier.

Satisfied and proud of doing something right for once, I got comfortable on the couch and drifted asleep.

I woke up to the sound of someone clearing their throat and blinked a few times to clear the sleep from my eyes.

Standing across from me was Stan. Beat red, looking more uncomfortable than I'd ever seen anyone before, Stan.

I struggled to sit up and felt the chill on my skin when the blanket slid down. At some point, I must've gotten too hot last night and taken my sweater off. It was tossed on the floor in front of me.

I was about to say something, but then I heard Henry shift on his bed. He sat up, rubbed the sleep from his eyes, and then his jaw dropped in disbelief.

I followed where his eyes dropped and found that my left tit had popped out of my tank top and was hanging freely for everyone to see.

Lovely. Just freaking lovely.

HOLIDAY HIJINKS

<u>Six</u>
Holly

I spent the majority of the morning hiding out in the garage as I tried to avoid seeing Henry's parents after the whole tit-gate scandal this morning. I was mortified the moment I realized what had happened and fled the room before anyone could say anything.

An hour had passed, and Henry hadn't bothered to come check on me yet. He sent a few text messages, but other than that—nothing.

I couldn't blame him; I mean, I flashed his very prim and proper father my breast as if I were some girl trying to get beads at Mardi Gras. I had already embarrassed him more than once, but this time it took the cake.

There was the sound of voices outside, and I sighed a breath of relief that they were all gone for now. I pulled on my only other pair of shoes—also knee-high boots with stiletto heels, but in brown leather instead of black—and headed to the kitchen.

I was starving but I wasn't about to cook for everyone again. Hell, I wasn't even going to cook for myself. I rummaged through the bags of nonperishable groceries Henry had brought but didn't unpack and found a box of organic energy bars he loved.

Knowing he wouldn't miss one, I took it out of the wrapper and quickly scarfed it down. I looked around for a coffee pot but not finding anything. Before I could look further, I heard the front door open, and voices floated through. I finished chewing my bite quickly, cursing when I accidentally bit the inside of my cheek, and then swallowed.

I rounded the corner to the living room at the same time Stan was heading toward the bathroom. I stepped to the side, moving out of his way, my face blushing red when I remembered the unfortunate incident from earlier. I didn't have to ask whether Margaret had heard about it, given the daggers she was shooting at me at the moment.

Henry sat down on the small couch he slept on last night and motioned for me to join him. Before I sat down, I noticed the fire was dwindling.

"Do you want me to add another log to the fire?" I offered, feeling the heat of his mother's glare on the back of my head.

"I can do it," he said, getting up.

"I know how to do it," I said flatly, blowing out a breath of frustration. "I did it last night after you fell asleep and nothing terrible happened."

I heard his mom clear her throat and ignored it.

"Okay, sure."

I smiled and turned around, ignoring the way my fingers trembled as I reached into the basket to grab another log.

Henry jumped forward, holding his hand out to stop me.

"What are you doing?!"

I pulled back in surprise and looked at him. *Had we not just talked about this?*

"I'm adding a log to the fire…" I said slowly, just in case he was having trouble processing things this morning without coffee.

He pinched the bridge of his nose and closed his eyes.

"Please tell me you didn't use those logs for the fire last night."

I looked at them and then at the other pile stacked tightly and piled high in a hole in the wall beside the fireplace.

I could feel my heart hammering in my chest.

"Holly," he pressed. Standing up to join me in front of the fire. "Which logs did you use last night?"

I discreetly pointed in the direction of the logs in the basket.

"What did I do wrong?" I whispered, not wanting to draw his mother's attention any more than I had already.

She stood up behind me and pointed at the logs.

"Those aren't for the fire. They're logs that have had names and special dates carved into them from many generations." She smugly looked down into the basket and shook her head. "At least they *were*."

She left the room, and I let out the shaky breath I'd been holding.

"Henry, I'm—"

He lifted his hand to stop me.

I pressed my lips together and closed my eyes. When I

opened them again, Henry was gone.

Twenty minutes passed without anyone returning to the living room, so I grabbed Henry's car keys and went outside to get some fresh air. If anything, I could sit in the SUV and listen to music. At least I wouldn't be in anyone's way, and there was nothing I could destroy.

I stepped outside and gasped at the bitter cold that nipped at my nose. I definitely didn't pack enough warm clothes for this weather. Thankfully we were spending our time inside, warm by the fire that was burning the precious memories that had been engraved onto the logs I had so absentmindedly thrown into the fire.

I walked around, enjoying the way the snow crunched beneath my heels, but reminded myself to be careful that I didn't slip and fall. The last thing I needed right now was broken bones or a trip to a hospital, given that I couldn't imagine one was close by. I scanned the area around me and felt an eerie chill when I realized that there was *nothing* close by. Not even another cabin if we needed help.

While I had taken the time to google what to wear in the wilderness, I hadn't bothered looking up what kind of animals to expect. There were large prints in the snow on the side of the house that seemed to go deep into the woods. Whatever it was, I was pretty sure I didn't want to meet it up close and personal.

Deciding that I'd already roamed too far, I turned to head back inside when I heard voices on the other side of the house. I stepped lightly and watched my footing until I was close enough to listen to what they were saying.

"What are you even doing with her, son?" Stan asked, his words sending knives straight to my heart. "I know you've been with her for a while, but you can't honestly tell me that you see yourself settling down and starting a life with her."

"I don't know," Henry answered. "Things have been rough for a few months now, and I thought that if I brought her up here for a weekend away that it might be the reset that we needed."

Reset? What in the world was he talking about?

I stepped closer, pulling down branches of the tree in front of me so I could hear better.

"I think you need more than a weekend."

"I know. I just didn't want to give up on us so easily, you know? It's been five years, dad. How did I not see that it wasn't working for me before now?"

A tear slid down my cheek and froze before it could make it all the way down.

"You've been busy with work and setting up your future. Sure, Holly has been fun, and I'm sure it's been nice having her at your house for some companionship, but she's not wife material. Just look at all the blunders she's made in the twenty-four hours she's been here. You can do better, I hate to say it."

"Yeah, I know." Henry exhaled heavily. "I actually met someone at work. I've been trying not to act on the chemistry between us, but it's hard not to when I don't feel the same heat between Holly and me anymore. It's like whatever we had when we first started dating has just fizzled and died. We've been together so long, but I can't imagine spending the rest of my life like this—with someone who will never live up to our family's standards."

"We have a reputation to uphold," Stan agreed firmly. "It would suit you well to find someone more within our class, so to speak."

"I don't know how I'm going to end it with Holly without her losing her mind. I guess maybe I brought her up here to buy some time. Give her one last weekend together before I break up with her."

"Is she going home for Christmas?"

"I doubt it. She doesn't talk to her family anymore, which has made it harder for me to do this. I know how much she clings to me and what she thinks we have together. It's like she's a frail person who can't function independently without someone holding their hand."

"Well, I can't help with that. But my recommendation is to rip the band-aid off now. Do it before you get back to the city. Then you can come spend Christmas with your mom and me in Texas on the ranch."

"I didn't even get her a gift yet," Henry said with a lack of emotion. "I know she's had her shopping done for months, but I haven't bothered looking for her. Maybe I knew all along that we wouldn't be together for Christmas?"

My body trembled as I stood there and listened. In an instant, the world around me started to crumble.

Here I had thought that he was bringing me up for a romantic weekend getaway so he could propose to me when in reality, he brought me here to see if there was anything worth trying to save before he broke up with me.

I turned to leave, having heard enough when I tripped over a low tree branch and snapped it. The sound was loud enough to get Henry and Stan's attention as they whipped around and caught me.

"Holly—" Henry said, his face turning red with embarrassment.

"Don't." I held my hand up. "If you want to break up with me, fine. I'm gone. I deserve better than this, anyway. Maybe you'll actually be able to satisfy the girl at work because you sure as hell haven't been hitting the mark with me."

I knew it was a low blow, but I didn't care at that point. It wasn't like he'd tried to spare my feelings, even though he didn't know I was listening.

He took a few steps toward me, but I shook my head and stormed off. There was nothing left to say—he'd already said it all; he just didn't know I had heard him.

What was I going to do anyway? Beg him to reconsider? Ask him to love me again when apparently he had already fallen out of love with me? He'd admitted that he had already met someone who gave him something I didn't—a spark. Chemistry. There was nothing left to try to save, and we both knew it.

I still had Henry's keys to his SUV in my pocket, so I dug them out, unlocked it, and climbed inside. I didn't give it a second thought as I started the engine and put it in drive.

The window was covered with snow and ice, which made it hard to see anything in front of me. But I didn't have time to stop and worry about scraping the ice off. The last thing I wanted right now was to see Henry or his parents. I drove slowly, praying that I didn't hit anything as I cranked the heater up to full blast and turned the defrosters on.

Things were going okay as I gripped the wheel tightly and

shivered against the cold leather seat. I didn't want to turn the seat warmers on until after I could get the windows cleared, so that meant I was going to freeze my ass off for a few minutes.

Thankfully I was in the middle of the woods and didn't have to worry about other vehicles right now. Soon a small patch of the window was clear at the bottom, so I leaned down and kept driving now that I could see what was in front of me.

I don't know how far I'd gotten before more than half of the window was clear, but I was happy that I could see and that there was no sign of Henry coming after me. Not that he had any reason to—this was what he wanted, after all.

My stomach turned, and I started crying again, trying to wipe the tears away as quickly as possible so they didn't blur my vision. I needed to focus on driving so I could get the hell out of there.

I was finally gaining some confidence in handling the SUV in the terrible weather, even with the snow falling faster than I could clear it with the wiper blades. I held my breath and kept my foot over the brake in case I needed it. Suddenly, a large animal darted out in front of me, and instead of hitting the brake, my foot tapped the gas. Realizing my mistake, I quickly reached over and slammed on the brakes, not remembering that I was technically driving on a sheet of ice.

There was no traction as the SUV spun wildly out of control. I pulled the wheel in every direction I could to keep the vehicle on the road but watched in horror as it plummeted down the side of a hill and straight into a tree.

<u>Seven</u>
Blake

I was busy splitting logs for firewood when I heard the sound of metal crunching in the distance. Luna's head whipped up, and I knew she heard it too.

"Let's go check it out." I set my ax down on the stump and started walking with her leading the way.

We walked a few miles with the snow whipping around me. I pulled the beanie down lower on my head and adjusted the insulated face covering I had on. I followed the sound of the horn blaring and discovered an expensive SUV stuck headfirst into a large pine tree.

I circled around to the driver's side and found a mess of blonde hair covering the steering wheel.

I knocked on the window, hoping they weren't dead. I really didn't feel like dealing with that today.

A few seconds passed, and nothing.

I pulled my glove off and knocked louder.

Suddenly the head lifted, and a very dazed looking—yet beautiful—woman looked up at me.

I used my finger to motion for her to roll the window down.

Once it was at least halfway, I leaned in and spoke loudly

to try to be heard over the horn.

"Do you think you can lean back so the horn will stop blaring?" I yelled, startling Luna beside me.

She seemed a bit dazed and confused but did as I asked.

I shook my head, trying to get my ears to stop ringing. Not wanting to scare her, I reached up and pulled the face mask off so she could see that I wasn't some creepy killer from one of those horror flicks everyone obsessed over.

"Are you okay?" I asked, pulling her attention back to me.

"You look like a lumbersnack," she whispered, her brown eyes dancing with delight.

"I'm sorry, a what?"

"A lumbersnack."

"What's that?" I asked though I wasn't sure I wanted to know.

"It's like a lumberjack that you want to eat. You know, like a gingerbread man. But yummier."

I raised an eyebrow, wondering how bad of a concussion she had.

"Do you think you can turn off the car?" I asked, ignoring her lumbersnack comments.

"Huh?"

"Turn off the car." I held my hand up and made the motion for her. I would've climbed in on the passenger side and done it myself if the whole front end wasn't crunched up like an accordion. It was going to be a big enough challenge getting her out of the vehicle.

She reached over and turned the ignition off and then leaned back against the seat again.

"Can you unlock the doors?"

She seemed to be a little more aware than a few minutes ago and did what I asked without any additional demonstration from me.

I grabbed the handle and tried to pull but didn't have any luck. The frame was completely bent, and the doors had been jammed.

"I'm not going to be able to get you out through the door, so you're going to have to climb out of the window. Okay?"

Her eyes widened as she stared at the small opening.

"You should be able to roll it down the rest of the way," I added. "I'll help you out."

"Okay," she said nervously and finished rolling it down.

"Are you hurt at all?" I asked, not trusting that she would really know whether or not she was. If anything, she would be in shock, and injuries wouldn't make themselves obvious until later.

"I don't know. I don't think so."

"Do you think you can lift yourself enough to get your upper body out? I can pull you through."

She looked down at her feet and wiggled them free.

"I think so."

I waited for her to get situated and then stepped to the side as she stuck her head through the window. She seemed uncertain as she reached for my shoulders and allowed me to hold her waist as I gently pulled her through.

Once she was out, I kept my grip on her until she could stand on her own. She smiled a nervous smile and stepped away, her knees instantly buckling beneath her.

I reached out and grabbed her, looking down to find the culprit for her falling.

"Son of a bitch," she grumbled, looking down at the bottom of her boot that was missing the heel. "Not another one."

I eyed her suspiciously, wondering why anyone in their right mind would be wearing boots like that in this kind of weather.

"I take it this has happened before?" I asked, my arm still wrapped around her small waist.

"Unfortunately, yes. Guess I won't be buying that brand again," she scoffed. "Someone is going to get a bad review when I get home."

"Okay," I said, ready to change the subject. "Do you have anything in the car that you need before we go?"

She shook her head no.

"Where are we going?" she asked.

"Back to my place."

She held a hand up and placed it firmly on my chest.

"What? I'm not going back to your place with you."

I frowned.

"Why not?"

"Because I'm not that kind of girl, you asshole."

I sighed heavily and shifted my weight. It was getting colder as the temperatures dipped with the heavy snow that was falling.

"I don't care what kind of girl you think you are, but you're about to be a frozen dead girl if we don't get moving."

I let go of her, making sure she was steady on her feet for a few minutes as I put my face mask back on. She wasn't dressed for this weather, and it was at least a few miles away from my cabin. Carrying her back would be enough of a workout to keep me warm, so I shrugged out of my flannel coat and held it out to her.

She was shivering and looked terrified as she took it.

"Look, we don't have time to stand here and talk about this. That storm is moving in quickly, and if we don't get back to my cabin, neither of us are going to survive the night. So, we need to get going now."

"But I don't know you," she whispered.

"Then I guess it's either trust me not to kill you or risk surviving out here."

Luna chose that moment to howl in the distance, striking fear in the woman's eyes.

"Alright, fine. I guess I have no choice," she said stubbornly.

"Put the coat on. It'll keep you warm."

"I'll be okay, thank you."

I worked my jaw back and forth in frustration.

"Just put the damn thing on," I growled.

Her eyes widened, and I thought maybe my tone had gotten to her. But then I followed where she was looking and spotted Luna.

"There's a wolf," she hissed without moving her mouth.

Luna moved forward, her eyes fixated on the woman. She let out a low snarl and showed her teeth.

"Sit, Luna."

I kept my eyes on the woman, knowing that Luna would immediately obey me.

"That was amazing," she whispered. "How did you do that."

"Basic dog commands. We need to get going."

"That's not a dog," she stuttered, looking down at Luna, who was still sitting.

"I'm going to carry you back," I said, ignoring her rambling about how huge Luna was. "We don't have much time—"

"I can walk," she interrupted.

I looked down at her shoes and then met her eyes.

"Fine," she sighed and looked away.

I debated on the easiest way to get her back without causing either of us too much strain.

"Ready?" I asked.

"As ready as I'm ever going to be."

I nodded, then lifted her over my shoulder and commanded Luna to follow me.

 It was a long trek back, but I kept my pace and adjusted her a few times as needed. Once we got within a few yards, I set her on her feet and slowed down so she could keep up. The storm had already dropped at least six inches while I was gone, and it was just the beginning.

HOLIDAY HIJINKS

Eight
Holly

"How's your head feel?" he asked, holding out a bottle of water and two Tylenol.

"Like I whacked it on a steering wheel," I joked, taking them from him. I took a sip and tossed back the pills, hoping they would numb something—anything would work at this point.

He sat on the arm of the leather chair across from where I was sitting on the couch, studying me carefully.

"So, what happened out there?"

I closed my eyes and willed myself not to cry. He was a stranger who was stuck with an injured crazy woman he didn't even know their name.

"I was trying to leave."

"Leave? Where?"

"I don't know. Anywhere but where I was."

"Why?"

I sucked in a deep breath and exhaled slowly through my nose.

"I was spending the weekend with my boyfriend at his family's cabin, and everything that could go wrong did.

And now I'm stuck in some stranger's cabin with a possible concussion and no way to get home."

"I'm Blake."

"Holly."

He stood up and walked into the kitchen, which was part of the living room. The cabin appeared to be close to the same size as Henry's family's but felt larger, with the two rooms combined as one instead of separated. There were wood floors, though these ones were more scuffed up, and the rugs appeared to be used and not just decorative.

Large windows framed the room with minimal decoration on the walls. It was obvious that he lived here and wasn't caught up in the appearance of his living space but in the functionality.

I leaned back against the cushion and pulled my feet under me to warm up. He'd helped me out of my boots as soon as we got in and left them on the mat by the door to dry, though he said I wouldn't be going anywhere any time soon with the storm that was rolling in.

The snow fell heavily around us in a blanket so thick that you couldn't see the trees through it. It would be a beautiful image if I weren't stranded and inconveniencing the lumbersnack who had to carry me for miles back to his cabin. If I wasn't making life hard for Henry and his family, then I was apparently destined to do it to Blake.

He returned a few minutes later with a coffee mug and extended it to me.

I carefully grabbed it, making sure not to spill as I sat up.

"It's hot chocolate," he announced as he watched me stare into the cup.

"You made me hot chocolate." I chewed the inside of my cheek to keep from crying.

"Yeah…"

He lifted his mug to his lips and took a drink.

He didn't strike me as the kind of guy who drank hot chocolate. Maybe it was the way he sat on the arm of the chair again like he was too manly to sit down and get comfortable. Or perhaps it was the way his hand wrapped tightly around the mug with little effort, showing the strength in his hands. It could've been his rugged good looks or his strong jawline that was covered in a neatly trimmed beard. Either way, it was his dark eyes that studied me under his thick brows that made me nervous. He had yet to take his beanie off his head, but I would be willing to bet that he had unruly hair that begged to be touched.

I shook my head to clear my thoughts and took a sip.

"Thank you for the hot chocolate," I said, holding it between both hands as I let it warm me up.

He gave me a curt nod but said nothing before tossing the rest of his back and emptying the cup.

I raised my eyebrows in surprise, wondering how in the hell he didn't burn himself.

"I'm going to go get more wood for the fire."

He got up and took his cup to the kitchen sink before snapping his fingers down by his side.

The dog that had startled me in the woods got up from the

rug she was lying on and followed him out the door before he pulled it shut behind them.

Once I was alone, I tried to relax and let everything that had happened in the last forty-eight hours process through my mind. It was still boggling to me that I had left for the trip so excited to go home an engaged woman, and now I was stranded with a stranger and unofficially single.

The headache that started a while ago was getting worse, and I began to feel nauseous. I knew it was likely because I hadn't eaten anything since the protein bar I'd stolen from Henry this morning, but I wasn't about to make myself at home and go rummaging through his cabinets.

I pulled my phone out of my pocket and tried to get a signal so I could get a ride back to LA. Not that I had a place to stay once I got there, but that was a problem to solve another day.

The door opened and brought in a gush of cold air. Blake pushed it closed with his heavy boot and dropped an armful of wood into the basket on the floor next to the fireplace.

"There's no internet here," he said curtly, nodding to my phone.

"Oh." I frowned and pouted my lips. "I was hoping to get an Uber back to LA."

He was bent over, arranging the firewood before tossing a few into the fire and then closing the screen.

"You're not going to find an Uber out here. Even if there were internet, getting to LA would cost you a fortune. Plus, that storm isn't letting up anytime soon, so you might as well get comfortable. You'll be staying a few days at minimum."

"I can't do that," I said, standing up and immediately felt the pain radiate up my leg and back. When I'd crashed the SUV, the impact of it not only broke the heel of my boot but also left my ankle sore and achy.

He reached out a hand and steadied me.

"Can you stand on your foot?" he asked, ignoring my objection.

"I think so."

"Let me see."

He was still holding onto me as he waited for me to put weight on it.

I rolled my eyes and let go of him as I tried. Slowly I pushed down, swallowing the cries of pain that wanted to escape.

"Sit down," he commanded, pointing to the couch as he helped me over.

I did as he asked and knew it was worse than I thought.

He sat on the edge of the wooden coffee table, gently brought my foot up, and placed it on his thigh.

"Can I take a look?" he asked, his fingers hovering over the bottom of my jeans.

"I don't think you'll be able to see much. My jeans are pretty tight."

He nodded and slowly pulled them up as far as they would go. Then he gently grabbed the top of my ankle sock and pulled it down, exposing my foot which was already shades of blue and purple.

"You definitely sprained it, but you might have a fracture or small break."

"Great," I mumbled. "What am I supposed to do now?"

"First, change out of the tight clothes you're wearing. Then you'll need to rest it and keep any weight off of it."

"I don't have anything to wear. Everything I had is back at my boyfr—*ex-boyfriend's* cabin." Not like I had packed anything loose to wear there either, but the point was that I literally had nothing but the clothes on my back.

"You can borrow something of mine."

I eyed him suspiciously, knowing that anything he had would fall right off of me, given his large frame and muscular body.

"Trust me. You'll be fine."

He got up, went to his bedroom, and returned a few minutes later with a stack of folded clothes.

"I can help you to the bathroom so you can change," he offered.

I nodded and accepted his hand as I stood up. He wrapped one arm around my waist and assisted me the short distance down the hall.

"Do you need help with the rest?" he asked, seeming slightly uncomfortable.

"No, thank you. I think I can manage."

He gave me another nod and pulled the door closed.

I exhaled heavily and tried to focus on the task at hand and not the way my body felt when he touched me.

I sat on the edge of the bathtub and slid my jeans off, being mindful of both my ankle and the bruising that still hurt from the fall in the garage. At first, I'd felt uneasy about wearing his clothes, but when I pulled on the black sweatpants, I felt so comfortable that nothing else mattered. I stripped off the sweater I was wearing, as well as the tank top underneath, and pulled the hoodie over my head.

I immediately felt more comfortable and warmer than I'd been all weekend. I wasn't trying to impress him, so to speak, but that didn't stop me from stopping in front of the bathroom mirror to fix my hair and try to freshen up.

A gasp escaped my lips when I noticed the red gash on my forehead from where I'd hit my head on the steering wheel. There were streaks of blood that had been wiped into my blond hair and a bruise almost as dark as my eyes.

No wonder he was taking pity on me—I looked like the trainwreck that I was.

A few seconds later, there was a knock on the door.

"Everything okay in there?" he asked.

I hopped slightly, keeping my weight off my foot while holding onto the wall. I opened the door and stepped to the side.

"Yeah, just peachy." I tried to smile, but it was pointless.

His eyes searched my face, and I noticed little golden flecks in the dark brown I hadn't seen before. They were pretty. I tilted my head and kept staring, feeling transfixed on them.

"Let's get you off of your feet." He wrapped his arm around my waist and pulled mine up over his shoulder as he guided me back to the couch.

Once I got settled, he handed me the throw blanket from the back of the couch, lifted my foot, and rested it on a stack of pillows. An ice pack was planted on top and then covered with a towel wrapped around it to keep it in place.

"You didn't need to go through all of this trouble," I said, feeling bad that he had to take care of me. "Thank you."

"Not a problem," he mumbled as he walked into the kitchen. "Do you eat meat?"

I turned and looked at him.

"I'm sorry, what?"

"Meat," he repeated, standing with the fridge wide open as he stared at me. "Do you eat it?"

"Yeah…"

He nodded his signature nod and then went about his business in the kitchen while I sat on the couch and watched some movie that was on the TV.

An hour later, my stomach growled as a heavenly aroma floated in from the kitchen. Blake came in from the kitchen, carrying two plates of food that he set down on the coffee table before helping me adjust so I could eat.

"Thank you so much for dinner," I said, excited to dive in.

"It's nothing fancy."

I smiled and took the time to check him out as he shuffled

about around me. I let him move my foot and noted the gentle way he'd set it on the pillow he'd placed on the floor for me to rest it on.

He wasn't wearing the beanie anymore, and I was right about his unruly hair. It was long, but not long enough to put in a man bun, though he didn't strike me as the kind of guy who would wear one even if he could. It was the perfect length to run my fingers through, and fell in his eyes as he leaned down to adjust the pillow.

Having him kneel in front of me while his hands gently touched my body was electrifying, and I wondered what it would feel like if he were doing something other than tending to my injured foot.

Before I was ready for the daydream to end, he pulled away and sat beside me on the couch. I was ready to lean forward to eat but was surprised when he lifted the top and it extended into a table so we didn't have to.

"Wow, that's a fancy table you've got there," I said, offering him the first genuine smile I'd had all day. "Where did you get it?"

Now that I was going to be starting over, it wouldn't hurt to get some functional furniture for wherever I ended up next.

"I made it," he said, glancing at me and then turning back to his food.

My jaw dropped as I turned fully to look at him.

"You *made* this? It's amazing!"

"Thank you."

He was constantly short with me, and I realized that it

wasn't anything I'd done wrong; it was just his personality. I didn't continue to bug him about the table since he seemed a little uncomfortable with my praise.

I lifted my fork and pierced a piece of potato. It was a simple meal of steak and potatoes, but it was amazing. I hadn't realized how quickly I was devouring it until I felt his eyes on me.

"Sorry," I said, covering my mouth to hide the bite I was still chewing. "This is delicious."

"I'm glad you like it."

"I was starving," I laughed, setting my fork down on the now empty plate.

He finished his last bite, set his down too, and turned to face me.

"You should have said something. There's plenty of food."

I felt my face redden with embarrassment and looked away.

"Look," he said with a sigh, pushing the top of the table down. "We're going to be together for a few days, maybe a week or longer. You're going to have to get comfortable helping yourself to whatever you want around here. I don't mind cooking, but you need to tell me when you're hungry."

"It's not a big deal, really."

"No," he said more aggressively. "It is. There is no reason to sit here and be hungry when there's plenty to eat. Consider this place your home until the weather clears and you can go home. You don't need to tiptoe around and act like you're an inconvenience."

"But I am!" I blurted out, shocked by my own outburst. "I can't remember the last time I didn't feel like I was inconveniencing someone in the past forty-eight hours."

He leaned back against the couch and relaxed for the first time I'd seen since I got there.

"Come on. It couldn't have been that bad."

I shifted as much as possible, got comfortable, and then recounted the events that had happened once I set foot inside Henry's family's cabin.

He winced when I told him about the fall in the garage, cringed when he heard about me using the dead grandmother's wedding veil as a table runner, and burst out laughing when I got to the part about my boob falling out of my tank top and flashing Henry's father.

"Okay, that's bad," he admitted, a smile still teasing his lips.

He had a great smile, and I wanted to see more of it.

"So see, I don't want to cause any more trouble. I just want to get out of here and get back to LA as soon as possible, so I'm not in anyone's hair."

"What are you going to do once you get back?" he asked.

"I honestly don't know," I admitted sadly.

I had also told him about Henry's confession to his father about breaking up with me and being interested in someone that he works with. Talking to Blake felt different. Liberating. And suddenly, I found myself not in a hurry to get back to LA anytime soon.

HOLIDAY HIJINKS

<u>Nine</u>
Blake

As the evening progressed, I noticed that Holly seemed to be more uncomfortable and achier, even though she wouldn't say anything. I'd kept up on giving her Tylenol and Ibuprofen to help with the swelling in her ankle but didn't know about her other fall until she told me at dinner. To say she'd had a rough few days was an understatement.

I cleaned up after dinner and then decided to run a hot bath for her. I didn't bother asking first because I knew she would fight me on it.

Once it was ready, I went into the living room and held out my hand for her.

"What are you doing?" she asked, lifting hers to mine.

I gently pulled her up, making sure to keep her weight off of her foot.

"I ran you a bath so you can soak."

"What?" She pulled her head back in disbelief. "You didn't have to do that."

"I know. I wanted to."

"But what if you need to use the bathroom?"

I frowned and looked down at her.

"I'll go outside."

She hesitated for a moment, not letting me move her toward the hallway.

"But it's cold out. It's snowing. I mean, it's practically a blizzard out there."

I nodded, still not understanding what the problem was.

"I'm not going to tie up your bathroom and force you to pee in the woods during a blizzard, Blake."

She tried to plant her hand on her hip but lost her balance and fell into my chest.

I caught a whiff of the shampoo she used in her hair and tried not to focus on the light citrus smell.

"I hate to break it to you, but I've peed outside in worse. Trust me, I'll be fine."

"But—"

"Holly, it's fine."

She snapped her cute little mouth shut and allowed me to help her to the bathroom.

Once we got in there, I debated how to get her into the tub without her putting weight on her foot. I wasn't sure that it was broken, but I also wasn't sure that it wasn't. At this point, I wanted to err on the side of caution since it would be hell to try to get her to a hospital in town with the storm raging outside.

"Thank you, I appreciate you doing this for me," she said softly.

"No problem," I mumbled as I shuffled around her to get into a better position. "Umm, if you want to get undressed, I can look away and then help you in once you're ready."

Her cheeks flushed pink as she looked at the tub and then back up at me.

She pulled her lower lip between her teeth while she debated.

"Okay."

I made sure she was steady and wasn't going to fall before I turned and faced the wall to give her some privacy. A few minutes later, I heard her clothes drop to the floor and tried not to focus on her being naked.

"Alright, I'm ready." There was a hesitancy in her voice.

I kept my eyes on hers as I wrapped my arm around her waist and held onto her with both hands as she did her best to climb in. I guided her the best I could and then bent down and lowered her into the water.

I had taken the time to add some Epsom salts to the water as well as some bubble bath my sister had left behind the last time she was here, which I was thankful for as she sank beneath the bubbles.

"Is the temperature okay?" I asked, hoping it hadn't gotten cold in the time it took from when I started it to when she got in.

"It's perfect, thank you."

"Alright," I said, clearing my throat. The way she looked at me as her naked body hid from my view made me think things I shouldn't. "Just yell for me when you're ready, and I'll come help you out."

"Okay."

She smiled, and that was my cue to get the hell out of there.

An hour later, I heard her soft voice calling my name and went to the bathroom to help her out of the tub.

She was still sitting in the water, only this time, there were no bubbles to hide her naked body. I immediately looked away, trying not to be disrespectful. I grabbed the clean towel I had set out for her earlier and tucked it under my arm.

"You ready?" I asked, unsure of where to look.

"Yes, please."

I struggled to figure out how to get her out of the damn tub without seeing her body, but it didn't seem like it would be possible. I shuffled the towel from one hand to the other before finally giving up and setting it down on the toilet.

"Blake?"

"Yeah," I stuttered, staring at the wall.

"It's fine. It's just a body. If you can lean down some, I can try to push myself out of the water."

I swallowed hard, knowing she was right. It was just a body. I had done this before, and I could do it again.

Okay, so maybe I'd never done *this,* but I'd done other stuff that was similar, and that's what mattered.

I bent down and braced the sides of the tub as she wrapped her arms around my neck. Once she had a good hold, I wrapped one arm around her while I used the other to push us up. She was tiny, to begin with, but felt even smaller as I held her against me and pulled her wet body out of the water.

Once she was out and standing safely on the rug, I let out the breath I had been holding. It had been a while since I'd been responsible for helping someone, so I was worried I would screw up and hurt her more.

She was breathing heavily as her breasts heaved against my chest. I could feel the hardening of her nipples as they brushed against the material of my t-shirt. My arms stayed wrapped tightly around her waist while she didn't bother to remove hers from my neck. A heat spread through me, quickly sending a rush of blood straight to my cock, which was pressed tightly against my jeans.

I noticed the small gasp that pressed through her lips, knowing that she felt how hard I was for her.

My body reacted to hers in a way I hadn't ever felt with anyone before. This raw attraction made me want to rub my hands all over her before plunging inside and claiming her pussy as mine.

I wanted to tilt my neck and kiss the inside of hers, but then I felt her weight shift and remembered that I was supposed to be helping her out of the tub, not fucking her.

"I'm going to get the towel so you can get dried off, okay?" I asked, my voice strained.

She nodded.

I pulled one hand away from her and quickly reached for it. I wrapped it around her body the best I could without touching her. She giggled and took the ends from me as she secured it to her body.

She lowered her eyes and tucked a strand of hair behind her ear.

"I'll, um, leave and give you some privacy."

I spun to leave, but her voice stopped me.

"Do you think you can help me get dressed?"

I froze in place, unsure of what to do. There was something about the way she said it and how her voice changed that made me think there was something more to what she was asking.

"Please."

My heart hammered in my chest as my cock stirred at the thought of seeing her body again.

"Sure."

Ten
Holly

What the hell was I doing?!

I had never been braver in my life than I was when I asked Blake to help me get dressed. Could I do it on my own? Probably. Would it be easy? Not likely. Was it an excuse to get him to touch my naked body again? Absolutely.

I stood there, allowing him to hold me up while he debated his answer. I knew it was a gamble asking him to help me, but I also couldn't deny feeling something a few minutes ago when he was holding me. I mean, I *literally* felt it against my thigh.

Maybe I was just desperate and imagined that there was chemistry between us. Maybe his stunned silence was because I revolted him so much that he couldn't stand the thought of seeing or touching me again. Or maybe it was because he knew I was fresh off of a relationship that barely ended a few hours ago. It could be that I was just crazy and imagining Blake was interested in me, just like I thought Henry and I were on the path to getting engaged.

But then again, he was really, really hard when I brushed my nipples against this chest.

He swallowed hard, his Adam's apple bobbing up and down as he grabbed the clothes I'd dropped on the floor earlier. He set them neatly on the toilet and then turned to face me. We locked eyes, and I could see the struggle warring in his eyes.

Without saying a word, I unhooked the towel, spread it open, and then let it fall beside me.

I licked my lips, enjoying the liberating feeling that was washing over me. I'd never been this sexually open, but suddenly, I didn't care about Blake seeing me. In fact, I wanted him to want me the way I wanted him right now.

Maybe this was exactly what I needed to get over Henry. Another man to make me feel alive for a bit. A distraction while I was stranded in the mountains with a frightening blizzard outside.

I tried to focus on the empowerment I felt instead of the nerves that were pulsing through me.

His eyes darkened as they roamed over my body and then suddenly widened when they landed on my bruised hip.

Before I could say anything, he whipped around faster than one of those Cullen kids in *Twilight* and was bent down looking at it.

"You didn't tell me it was that bad, Holly."

"Honestly, I don't know how bad it is," I laughed. "I haven't really been in a position where I could see my own ass."

"It's bad."

I frowned and pouted my lips. Maybe I hadn't paid much attention to it because Henry hadn't made a big deal out of it either. I didn't want to be a crybaby, and it wasn't like there was anything anyone could do about it. It just needed time to heal.

"Well, that's not very nice. I've always been told I have a nice ass. Other guys seem to like it."

He ignored my joke and gently brushed his fingers across my skin, tracing the outline of where I was bruised to give me an idea of how big it was.

God, his touch was addictive. It was light and feathery to not hurt me, but even pressure to let me know he was there. And dear Lord, my body knew he was there.

Instinctively, I stepped to the side some on my good foot, allowing my legs to part. I could feel the heat of his breath against my thigh and trembled, imagining his face between my thighs. He was so close that I could almost feel it happening.

He looked up, and I knew he could see the desire etched on my face. Not only that, but my nipples were also hard again, and there was an aching in my core.

Not sure if he was getting the message about what I wanted, I reached down and gently grabbed his hand as his fingers trailed over my skin. Then, I slowly moved it over my hip and hissed out a breath as I skimmed it over my pussy.

He groaned as he pressed kisses to my leg as his finger trailed the inside of my lips. I wanted to open for him and let him know I was ready, but I couldn't stand on both feet. As if reading my mind, he picked me up, backed me against the wall, and then sunk to his knees again.

Without asking, he lifted my injured leg over his knee and then leaned in to lick my pussy as he held my body in place on the wall. *Henry had never done anything like this with me before. While he'd gone down on me a few times, it was always in bed with me on my back, and it never lasted more than a few minutes. I couldn't even remember the last time he made me come from oral sex. Hell, I couldn't remember the last time he made me come, period.*

I cried out as he licked again, spreading my folds with his tongue as it dipped inside and tasted me.

"Yes!" I panted, grabbing a handful of his hair and yanking as he pushed his face deeper into my pussy. I knew it would feel good between my fingers. He officially had sex hair because it was the perfect length to hold onto as I rode his face.

He reached up and pulled my other leg over his shoulder, holding my ass in place as I slid a little down the wall. He was still eating me, his tongue working its magic against my clit, when he slipped two fingers inside my folds.

I was close to the edge with the friction he was giving me and wanted to come right then and there. Suddenly, he curved his fingers inside, hitting a spot I never knew I had, and I could swear I saw stars. I bit down on my lip to keep from screaming as I rode his face during climax.

A few seconds later, I was still panting as he slowly removed his fingers and sat me down on the floor.

"That was amazing," I said breathlessly.

My head was spinning, trying to focus on what had just happened. I wasn't the kind of girl to just jump into bed with a guy she didn't know—or be pinned against the wall, for that matter. But something about this didn't feel wrong. It didn't feel dirty. It felt good, and I wanted more of it.

For once, I didn't want to stop and think about what I was doing. I wanted to act on impulse and see where it took me.

Again, it wasn't like Henry was out looking for me.

He nodded, breathing heavily himself.

"I want more."

His eyes widened and then roamed over my body again.

I glanced down and found that same bulge in his jeans that I had seen earlier.

"Just a fling, Blake. It doesn't have to mean anything other than two people who are horny and stuck together for a few days." I don't know who I was trying to convince more—him or me.

He licked his lips, and I prayed he was about to say yes.

My chest was still heaving as the blood flowed back through the rest of my body.

"I know you're hard," I said quietly. "Let me take care of you the way you just took care of me."

He shook his head and then got up and left.

I sat there for a few moments, trying not to cry as I processed his rejection. But then he returned a few minutes later with a stack of condoms in his hand, and I knew I was in for a good time.

He extended a hand and helped me up before setting me down on the vanity.

"Are you sure this is what you want?" he asked as he unzipped his jeans and started stroking his cock.

He wasn't wearing any underwear.

I nodded and chewed my lower lip.

Within seconds, he tore the condom open, slid it onto his penis, and then lined up his head at my entrance.

I spread my legs for him, showing him how wet he'd made me just a few minutes before. He rubbed my slit with his thumb and then pushed inside.

My head fell back as I moaned. He gripped my hips, pulled me further to the edge of the counter, and began thrusting.

He was big—freaking huge—as my pussy wrapped tightly against him. I wanted to take it in my mouth and suck him off, but this was just as good. I gasped when he leaned in and pulled a nipple into his mouth, nipping lightly before clamping down and sucking.

The friction felt so good as he rubbed against my clit while he fucked me, but combined with the nipple stimulation, I was ready to come again. I dug my nails into his hair and pulled tightly as we came undone together.

This was a high I had never been on before, and I wasn't ready to come down anytime soon.

<u>Eleven</u>
Blake

My mind was racing a mile a minute while my body hummed with satisfaction after being inside of Holly. I had no idea where in the world that came from, but I wasn't complaining.

That also didn't mean I wasn't sitting there next to her on the couch, wondering if I should have tried harder to say no. Not that I didn't find her attractive or that I didn't want to do it, but I wasn't the kind of guy who jumped a girl's bones less than twenty-four hours after her breaking up with someone. I had more class and respect than that, though I guess that wasn't really showing right now, was it?

An old black-and-white movie played on the TV, but neither of us was really watching it. I could see Holly's mind racing as she nervously chewed her nails. Her foot was propped up on my lap with another ice pack to reduce the swelling, and it took everything I had in me not to let my fingers trail up her leg and caress it.

She was wearing my sweats and hoodie again, and I had to admit—I kinda liked it.

It was getting late and we had yet to talk about sleeping arrangements. Once I saw how bad the storm was getting, I knew she would be staying with me for at least a few days, probably longer. There weren't any other options, even if she wanted to go back to her asshat of an ex-boyfriend's cabin—there was no way to get her there safely.

My cabin wasn't huge, but it was big enough for me. There was the guestroom that my sister stayed in when she came to visit, but the bed was old and needed to be replaced. I didn't want Holly to be in any more pain than she was already in, so I decided she'd sleep in my room, and I'd take the crappy bed.

When she yawned, that was my cue to get her settled.

"Ready to call it a night?" I asked, noticing the way her body was sinking into the couch as she relaxed.

"Yeah, I don't think I could stay awake right now if I tried," she laughed. "Is it okay if I sleep on the couch?"

"No." I frowned and shook my head.

Her head tilted to the side in confusion.

"You'll sleep in my bed, Holly. I'm not letting you sleep on the couch."

"Oh, no," she rushed out. "I couldn't do that. I'm fine on the couch, really."

I pinned her with a look that got her to snap her mouth close before she said anything more.

"You're not sleeping on the couch."

"I did at Henry's family's cabin, and it was actually comfortable."

"Well, I'm not Henry, and this isn't his pretentious family's cabin. You're sleeping in the bed."

She swallowed hard and started chewing her nails again.

"Um, where will you sleep?"

In bed beside you so I can roll over and make love to you throughout the night.

"There's a guest bedroom." I cleared my throat, pushing the dirty thoughts aside.

"Oh, why don't I take that room, so I don't put you out?"

I shook my head again.

"Why not?"

"Because, Holly, that bed sucks, and your body is seven shades of black and blue right now. You need to rest and let your body heal. You will sleep in my bed, which is the most comfortable option in the cabin."

I gently lifted her foot and then set it on a pillow as I got up and walked away, effectively ending the conversation.

I hurried to get the room set up for her and made sure I took what I needed to the guest room. There was only one pillow that I slept with; the rest were all brand new and never used. I tried to arrange them for Holly on the bed without looking like I was trying too hard. Not sure if she got cold easily, I grabbed an extra blanket from the closet and added it to the edge of the bed so she could use it if she wanted to.

I tossed the pillow onto the bed and grabbed an extra blanket. It wasn't a large room, but it had everything I needed, including a nightstand with a phone charger and a TV mounted on the wall in case sleep eluded me again tonight.

When I walked back into the living room, I found Holly asleep on the couch. I hadn't been gone that long, but she looked exhausted. I didn't want to wake her, but I knew she would be stiff and sore tomorrow if I let her sleep in that position, so I bent down, picked her up, and carried her to my bed.

Once she was settled and covered under the blankets, I grabbed her phone from the living room and put it on the charger beside her bed. I wanted to reach down and kiss her goodnight, but that felt really out of line, so I pushed that thought aside, closed her door, and pretended that I wasn't already starting to feel something for someone who was still a stranger.

The next morning, I was up before Holly. Probably because I had slept like shit the night before and didn't fall asleep until around two. I padded around the kitchen, starting a pot of coffee while I watched the snow falling outside.

It was going to be a brutally cold day. Thankfully I had planned ahead and brought in enough firewood to last a few days. Aside from taking Luna outside, there was no reason either of us would need to brave the storm.

I'd lived in Hope Valley for ten years and had never seen a storm this bad. Sure, we got plenty of snow each year, which brought in many skiers, but this was enough snow to shut down the slopes for a few days.

I was standing at the kitchen sink, drinking my coffee when I heard Holly coming down the hallway. I set it down and rushed to help her, so she didn't hurt herself.

"Hey, you should've called for me. I would have come and helped you."

"It's okay," she said softly. "My foot actually feels a lot better this morning. It doesn't hurt to walk on it."

I nodded and led her to the couch. She sat down and I

arranged a pillow for her to put her foot on.

"Do you mind if I look at it?" I asked, my fingers reaching to pull off her sock.

She nodded.

Slowly I pulled it down and cradled her foot in my other hand while I examined it. There was still some bruising, but overall the swelling had gone down. I turned it and looked at the other side, not noticing anything worrisome.

"I think it was a bad sprain," I said, continuing to check it out. "It doesn't look like anything is broken, and since you can walk on it without pain, I'd say it's a safe bet. However, sprains can be painful for a few days, so it's best to stay off your feet today and rest. I'll grab you some Ibuprofen and an ice pack."

"You don't have to keep taking care of me," she insisted, pulling her foot back after I set it down.

"I don't mind. But I'm serious—stay off of your foot. Unless you need to use the bathroom, there's no need to be on it."

"You sure seem to know a lot about it. Are you a doctor or something?"

I avoided looking at her as I got up and grabbed the first-aid kit from the kitchen.

"I was a medic in the Army."

"Army?"

I nodded and pulled out a roll of elastic bandage. I'd debated whether or not to wrap her foot last night but decided against it because of the amount of swelling she had. Now that the swelling had gone down, I wanted to make sure we kept some compression on it.

"Eight years. I got out ten years ago and moved to Hope Valley."

"Why did you leave?"

"My mother was sick, and I couldn't stand the thought of her dying while I was stuck somewhere overseas."

"I'm so sorry."

"Don't be. I got to spend the last few years of her life with her. Took care of her. After that, I realized that life is too short to spend doing something you don't want to."

I felt her eyes on me and looked up to find emotions flashing across her face.

"Being a medic was fine. I loved helping people. But at the end of the day, a career in the Army wasn't for me. I wanted to be on my own. Do what I wanted. Come and go as I pleased."

"So what do you do now? Are you like a real lumberjack?"

I chuckled and sighed.

"You mean *lumbersnack*?" I teased, looking up to meet her eyes.

Her brow furrowed in confusion.

"When I found you yesterday, the first thing you told me was that I looked like a lumbersnack. Kinda like a gingerbread man—"

"Oh my god!" She lifted her hands and covered her face

with embarrassment. "I thought I dreamt that!"

"Nope. It really happened."

"I'm so sorry," she apologized with a laugh. "I guess I hit my head harder than I thought."

"No need to be sorry. Though you are the first person to call me that."

"Well, I mean, you kinda looked like one with the beard and the flannel." She paused and looked down at Luna, who was sleeping on the rug by the fireplace. "And the pet wolf."

My cheeks split into a grin that I couldn't stop.

"You're half right about that. Luna is a Siberian Husky and wolf mix, though she's more husky than wolf."

"She's beautiful, but I'm not going to lie—I was sure I was going to shit my pants yesterday when I saw her."

I laughed and finished wrapping her foot.

"What do you feel like for breakfast?" I asked as I went to the kitchen and put the first-aid kit back where it belonged.

"You don't have to feed me," she insisted.

"I know I don't have to. Now, what do you want to eat?" I stood in front of her, arms folded over my chest.

She giggled and pulled the sleeves of my hoodie up to hide her mouth.

"What are my options?"

"Eggs, bacon, sausage, frozen hash browns, toast, and possibly a Pop-Tart. I need to check the stash of those, though."

I didn't eat Pop-Tarts, but my sister did, and I couldn't remember if there were any left after the last time she visited a few months ago.

"What are you going to eat?"

Her question was innocent enough, but that didn't stop my eyes from wandering hungrily to between her thighs, remembering the way she tasted last night when I ate her out against the bathroom wall.

Her brown eyes darkened, and her legs shifted slightly as if she was inviting me in for another taste.

"That depends on what *my* options are."

The tension palpitated between us as our eyes locked onto each other.

"You can have whatever you want."

"Whatever?" I confirmed, my voice deep and husky.

She nodded, her chest rising and falling rapidly as I approached her.

"In that case, I think I want to eat you again."

A small gasp escaped her full lips before she licked them and nodded as I leaned down to pull her sweats off.

I gently removed them, making sure not to hurt her, and then tossed them across the room. I snapped and pointed to my room, knowing that Luna would follow my command and leave. Next, I slowly pulled her panties off, taking my time teasing her as she wiggled anxiously beneath me.

Her legs fell open and welcomed me as I laid in front of her and got myself situated. I lifted her injured foot, rested it on my shoulder, and then added the other.

She giggled and tried to squirm, but I pinned her down with my body.

"You need to keep your foot elevated. Basic first-aid," I teased before dipping my head between her thighs and licking her lips.

She gasped and arched her back as her fingers grabbed my hair and pulled. God, I loved when she did that. I didn't usually keep my hair this long, but I was going to if she kept doing that.

I held her thighs in place while I teased her with my tongue, circling her clit before flicking it rapidly. She was already wet for me, and that made my dick achingly hard. I wanted to be inside her again, but I also couldn't get enough of this. I could eat her for every meal for the rest of my life.

She panted as I slid my tongue between her folds and fucked her with it. Keeping her injured foot braced on my shoulder, I lowered my other hand between her thighs and started to rub her clit while I continued thrusting two fingers deep inside.

"Fuck me," she cried out, her thighs squeezing my face as she came.

I sucked every last drop of wetness from her pussy and then came up for air.

"I plan to," I assured her with a wink.

I set her leg down gently, then ran off to grab a condom. I stripped down in the bedroom and rolled it on as I headed back to the living room.

She was still lying in the same position, looking completely sated and satisfied.

"You ready?" I asked, stroking my cock for her.

She nodded and licked her lips again.

"I want to taste you," she whispered. "I want that huge dick in my mouth."

I climbed on top of her, lining myself up at her entrance.

"It's a good thing we're snowed in with nothing else to do."

Before she could say anything, I pushed inside, closing my eyes as I went slowly to let her adjust to my size.

She was so fucking tight that it made me want to shoot my load that much quicker.

"Fuck me, Blake. Now," she urged.

Not needing any more encouragement, I pulled out and then slammed into her, groaning as she moaned my name.

Her pussy greedily clenched around my cock, milking every last drop of cum while I rubbed her clit with each thrust, making sure she came again too.

Her orgasms weren't quiet—which I loved. They were loud and sensual, and I couldn't get enough of them. I loved the way she scratched my back and clawed at my skin as if she needed it as much as I did.

Before pulling out, I gently cupped the side of her face and lowered my lips to her. We had fucked twice, and I knew what her pussy tasted like, but I had yet to kiss her. Once I did, I knew I would never want to stop again.

Twelve
Holly

The next few days were uneventful as the snow continued to fall, blanketing us inside the cabin. My foot had recovered enough to where I could put weight on it for short bouts of time, but Blake was adamant about keeping me off of it when he could. While sometimes that meant he was doing the cooking or cleaning for us, most of the time, it was an excuse for him to be between my legs—not that I was complaining.

I was only twenty-three, but Blake showed me more in the bedroom in three days than Henry had ever shown me in five years. He was my first, so it wasn't like I'd had anyone else to compare him to until now.

When we weren't busy humping like bunnies, we found different ways to kill time while cooped up inside. Which, honestly, wasn't that bad. While I loved life in LA and the constantly rushing around to auditions, I was actually enjoying my downtime with Blake.

He had a small collection of board games that we played when we needed a break from watching TV, which happened more frequently after I suggested a few rounds of strip Monopoly. Turned out Blake didn't mind making me homeless after I had to sell off all of my properties and beg him for a place to stay while I was naked and riding his cock.

It was four days until Christmas, and I was starting to stress about not getting back to LA. I hadn't mentioned it to Blake yet, but I felt bad that I was keeping him from whatever plans he might've had. While I had nothing going on back home for me, that didn't mean he didn't have a family he wanted to spend it with, without some strange woman intruding.

I sat on the couch and watched him throw a stick for Luna as she ran through the snow to fetch it. He was bundled up in a thick coat that made him look twice as large, and I wondered how easily he could move inside. It was bitterly cold out there, so I couldn't imagine they would be out there for long.

I was flipping through the channels, looking for something to watch, when the door opened, and Luna came rushing in, covered in snow. Blake came in behind her and shut the door before the heat escaped.

Luna shook in front of the fireplace, sending chunks of snow my way, before plopping down in front of the fireplace.

I squealed and held up the blanket to shield myself.

"Sorry, she loves the snow," Blake laughed, pulling off his beanie.

"I can see that," I laughed along with him.

Luna had grown on me during the time I'd spent with them, and she no longer came across as the scary giant wolf dog I initially thought she was. She was incredibly sweet, and an amazing dog that followed every command Blake gave her.

"What are you up to?" he asked as if there were that many options available.

"Nothing, just browsing through the channels."

"Do you want to help me outside?"

I turned the TV off and set the remote on the coffee table before pushing the blanket off of me and standing up.

"Sure." It didn't matter what he needed my help with; I was ready to do it.

"You're going to need some warmer clothes. I'll be right back."

He returned a few minutes later with a thick flannel coat that he helped me into, as well as a scarf, some gloves, and a face mask like the one he was wearing. Then he grabbed a pair of boots that were easily three times too big for me and helped me into them after adding a few pairs of socks to pad them so they wouldn't pull off.

"You ready?" He looked me up and down, answering for himself. "Let's go."

"Show me the way."

We stepped out into the cold, and Blake pulled the door closed behind us. I shivered and wrapped my arms around myself, wondering what in the world he could need help with out here. He'd already come out this morning to bring in more firewood.

"Don't worry, it'll be worth it," he shouted through the thick fabric covering his face as he tried to be louder than the wind whipping past us.

"Okay," I yelled back, following him into a small clearing beside the house.

He led the way, checking behind him every few feet to make sure I was still there. Finally, we were far enough away from the cabin that I couldn't see it anymore. I started to panic that we would get lost or stranded until I remembered Blake had lived here long enough to know which way was home.

Finally, he pulled me to the side and looked at the trees in front of us.

"Which one do you like?"

I tilted my head in confusion.

"You brought me out here to pick a favorite tree?"

The wind was quieter here because of the thick trees surrounding us, blocking it out.

"I brought you out here to help me pick a Christmas tree."

I tilted my head up and grinned at him, though he couldn't see it through my face covering. That certainly explained the ax I saw him bring with us. At first, I thought it was for protection in case we ran into a wild animal. Now it made much more sense.

"We're going to cut down a Christmas tree?!" I couldn't contain the excitement in my voice if I tried.

"Yup. Just pick one, and it shall be yours."

I looked around, trying to find the perfect one, touching each of the branches as I passed by. Suddenly I stopped. Standing before me was the *perfect* tree.

"That one," I said, pointing at it.

"Yeah?"

I stepped back and watched in awe as he got started. Luna waited patiently at my side, giving him the space he needed as the tree fell onto the ground on the other side.

I clapped excitedly when he was done and then helped him carry it back to the cabin. Thankfully it wasn't a huge tree and didn't need to be cut again once we got it inside. Blake grabbed the tree stand and got it secured while I held the tree in place.

He stood up and nodded for me to let go.

My heart raced wildly like a little girl in a toy store for the first time as I stared at the beautiful tree. It was tucked into the corner between two windows, making it the most gorgeous image I'd ever seen with the snow still falling outside.

"It's incredible," I whispered, continuing to stare in awe. "I could look at this every day."

The words escaped my lips before I could think about them.

"It's quite the beautiful sight, isn't it?"

The butterflies swarmed in my stomach when I noticed that he was looking at me, not the tree.

Thirteen
Blake

I'd never been one to put up a tree for Christmas. I just never saw the point since I spent the holiday alone. My sister was a traveling doctor and was usually somewhere international this time of year, so we stopped celebrating it together around the time my mother died. My dad was never in the picture, which left me with no other family to spend it with.

But seeing how Holly lit up seeing the tree made me want to do all of the things my mother used to do with us when we were little. Back when Christmas was a magical time of year. I'd tucked those feelings away for so long now that it felt weird letting them rise to the surface again. But as far as Holly was concerned, something was constantly growing around her. Usually my cock.

I went out and rummaged through the shed until I found the boxes marked *Christmas* in the back and brought them in. There were tangled messes of lights that we sorted together and then hung on the tree. Holly seemed to enjoy herself, so I didn't stop her from hanging them above the windows or throughout the rest of the cabin.

I was nervous about going through the box of ornaments with her, but we also needed to decorate the tree, so I sucked it up and plopped down on the floor beside her.

Her foot was ten times better than it was a few days ago, and I was glad to see that she wasn't in much pain from her fall, either. A little bit of rest and TLC seemed to be helping her.

"Did you want to go through them first?" Holly asked, sitting with her hands in her lap as I opened the lid to the box.

"Honestly, it's been so long since I've packed these away that I don't even remember what's inside." I shrugged.

"I don't want to intrude on something personal."

"I appreciate that. It's okay, let's go through them together."

She nodded and smiled softly as if she knew this might be hard for me.

The truth was that most of these were from my childhood and I'd packed them up and brought them home after clearing out my mom's stuff when she died. I had a great childhood, but I regretted the years I'd been away for Christmas, and she was left to decorate the tree and spend it alone.

My sister and I had tried to convince her not to go through all of the efforts of putting the tree up if it was just her, but she insisted that she enjoyed looking at it and that it reminded her of beautiful memories.

When I pulled the first ornament out, I felt a pain in my heart and knew exactly what she meant.

The fragile angel hung on a gold hook with frayed threads that looked like they would break at any moment. I continued to stare at it for a few minutes until I felt Holly's eyes on mine.

"My mom got this ornament when I was five, and my sister was two. My dad had just left, and she didn't have money to buy us gifts. One day while she was on her break at work, a man approached her. She was crying, upset that she couldn't get us anything, and he sat down and talked to her. It turned out that he owned a toy store a few blocks away and needed help with the holiday rush. My mom was working as a waitress at a diner and was stuck working the graveyard shift. She took the job he offered her, and he was so thankful for the help that he let her pick a toy for each of us, free of charge. When she'd finally chosen what she wanted, he added this ornament to her bag and told her it was her guardian angel. As long as she had it, she would never lose her way."

Her eyes welled up with tears as she listened to the story, reaching her fingers up to brush them away.

"He passed a few days later, but not before he promoted her to manager. His son took over the store and kept my mom there until she got too sick to work. It was the best thing that ever happened to her. I'd forgotten about this angel until now. My mom used to say that it was magical and would help those who had it find their way."

My throat burned as I fought back the tears.

"That's a beautiful story," she said, her face still wet.

I stood up and looked for a spot on the tree to hang it, making sure it wouldn't fall off and break if Luna bumped it.

We spent the next hour going through the ornaments and decorating the tree as we laughed and shared stories of our memories from Christmases growing up.

Once we were finished, we stepped back and looked at our masterpiece. It was beautiful, but not only that, it brought back a feeling that I thought had died inside. The only problem was that it wasn't the tree that made me feel alive again. It was Holly.

I made dinner while she flipped through my stack of DVDs, picking something for us to watch. It was weird how quickly we'd fallen into a routine with each other after only a few days, but everything with Holly felt right and oddly comfortable. It wasn't forced, and neither of us seemed to pretend to be something we weren't.

Holly devoured her bowl of fettuccini and then went for seconds while I sat on the couch and digested. While she was in the kitchen, her phone vibrated on the coffee table. I tried not to be nosey but seeing her ex-boyfriend's name on the screen made my stomach drop.

Why was Henry calling her? Was he just now getting around to checking on her? As far as I knew, this was the first time he'd bothered to reach out since she confronted him at his family's cabin after overhearing his plans to break up with her.

When she returned, her phone dinged to alert her to the new voicemail. I kept my eyes glued to the TV and acted like I hadn't seen anything.

Her brow furrowed as she pressed it to her ear and listened to the message.

"Everything okay?" I asked, still refusing to look at her or acknowledge I knew who had called.

She paused for a moment before setting her phone down and twirling her fork around her noodles.

"Yup."

We went to bed that night, both of us ignoring the new elephant in the room. I had hoped that she would tell me about Henry calling but I felt uneasy when she didn't bother to mention it. Was she planning to call him back when I wasn't around? What had he said in the message? My mind was spinning a mile a minute as I struggled with one dreadful thought—what if she goes back to him?

The next morning I woke up to the sun shining through the sheer curtains in my bedroom. We'd given up on sleeping in separate rooms after we kept banging nonstop, but last night I couldn't sleep knowing that she'd kept Henry's call from me.

Holly had been with me for almost a week, and we still hadn't talked about what would happen once the storm passed and the roads were clear enough for her to get back to LA. Maybe that was what the call was about. Had Henry offered to take her home? Was she going to take him up on it? There were so many unanswered questions that we needed to discuss, but I didn't know how without overstepping.

I was in the kitchen making breakfast when Holly came in after taking a shower. She hopped up onto the counter beside me, wearing another one of my hoodies and a new pair of sweats she found in my dresser. I'd told her to help herself to whatever she wanted but was glad she'd decided to forgo underwear since she only had one pair, and I conveniently kept forgetting to do laundry. Even though she was flirty and in a good mood, I couldn't shake the feeling that something was off. It was like I was just waiting for the other shoe to drop.

"Breakfast smells good," she said, smiling at me as I turned the sausage link in the pan.

"Thanks. It should be ready in a few minutes."

She frowned a little, obviously aware that something was off with me but not knowing what.

She got down and made herself busy with fixing our coffee for us. I joined her at the table a few minutes later and set her plate down in front of her.

I took a bite of my toast while she ate her scrambled eggs and looked out the window behind me.

"I can't believe the sun is finally shining," she commented with a huge smile.

"Yeah, they should have the roads clear soon." I didn't bother to turn around to see what she was talking about. It didn't matter how bright it was outside; it did nothing to ease the darkness that was seeping into my heart.

There was no use in beating around the bush. It wasn't like I could pretend she was still stranded and force her to stay with me if she didn't want to. For all I knew, she had a family waiting for her in LA that she needed to spend the holiday with. *Or Henry.* Christmas was only three days away, yet she hadn't mentioned what her plans were.

"Oh. Wow, that quickly?"

I couldn't tell if she was genuinely surprised or if I detected a hint of disappointment in her voice.

"They're pretty good at clearing it as soon as the storm passes."

I lifted my coffee to my lips and took a sip.

"I can drive you if you need me to."

She was mid-bite when she stopped, a panicked look on her face.

"Unless you wanted someone to come get you. It doesn't matter to me." I didn't bother to mention Henry's name, but the look that flashed across her face told me I was right about him.

I got up and took my plate to the sink before it could get any more awkward.

"I'm going to take a shower and clean up."

I felt like a dick for leaving her to finish eating by herself, but I didn't have a choice. I was already in too deep. I needed to separate myself from her as soon as possible. I was too old for her, and she was still in love with another man.

This was the reason I distanced myself from people and stayed to myself in the middle of nowhere, deep in the woods. Because allowing yourself to get close to someone meant that it hurt like hell when they walked away and left.

Fourteen
Holly

What the hell just happened?

I sat at the table by myself, trying to pick my jaw up off of the floor after Blake abruptly left. He'd been acting strange since last night, but today was even worse. It was like he'd gone back to the grumpy, cold Blake that I first met a few days ago.

I knew he had probably seen my phone last night when Henry called, but he didn't say anything. I wasn't sure whether to bring it up or not, but after seeing the way he worked his jaw while I listened to the voicemail, I decided not to.

It wasn't like Blake was a child who needed to be coddled—he was thirty-six and had probably been through his fair share of relationships and breakups. Granted, I was barely twenty-three, but I didn't feel like I was too young to know how to handle this one. Just because Henry called and asked me to call him back didn't mean I was going to. He hadn't bothered to check on me since I left, so as far as I was concerned, he could go kick rocks.

But I wasn't sure that it was just the call from Henry that was under his skin. When I mentioned that the weather had cleared, he seemed almost anxious to get me out of his cabin and back on my way to LA. Maybe I was hallucinating again and imagined that things were going better with Blake because *I* wanted them to be that good.

I wasn't going to beg anyone to want to have me around—not Henry, and sure as hell not Blake. If he didn't want me here, fine. I would find a way back to LA.

While he was in the shower—the longest one he'd taken since I'd been there—I searched for rides back to the city. I knew it would cost a fortune, and unless I maxed out every single one of my credit cards, I couldn't afford to do that.

Renting a car would be somewhat easier, but I still had to find a ride to the lot, which meant that I would have to find an Uber or ask Blake to take me. I really didn't want to inconvenience him, and then I read the fine print about there being a *young renter fee* for renters under twenty-five. That was going to get expensive as well.

There was only one option, and I hated to use it. Henry's voicemail said that he was catching a ride home with his parents today since I had taken his SUV and that he wanted to make sure I'd gotten home alright with the storm. He went on and on about being worried sick about me—*not so worried that he called before now*—and asked that I at least let him know that I was okay.

I groaned and then lifted my phone to my ear and pressed send.

Luna watched me from the rug in front of the fireplace, and I swear I could hear her snarling under her breath as if she knew what I was about to do.

"Holly," Henry breathed out as if it pained him not to hear from me.

"I need a ride. Your SUV is totaled and stuck in a tree."

"Okay. Okay, sure. Just tell me where you're at."

I sucked in a deep breath and pinched the bridge of my nose. I hated that I was going to have to ask Blake for his address so I could give it to my dumb ex-boyfriend.

When I opened my eyes, Blake was standing in front of me, drying his hair with just a towel wrapped around his waist.

"Holly?" Henry asked.

"Yeah. I'm still here."

"Okay, what's the address?"

I kept my eye's on Blake's and felt the knot in my stomach grow larger by the second.

"Ummm. I don't have it. Hold—"

Before I could say anything else, Blake reached out and snatched my phone from me.

He must've heard me ask for a ride and knew I didn't know his address.

He walked into the living room and faced the window as he rattled off directions. When he was done, he ended the call, and his fingers flew across the screen before he headed back to where I was sitting and handed it to me.

"He'll be here in thirty."

My heart beat wildly in my chest as my blood pressure rose. He walked off, closing his bedroom door behind him.

I looked at my phone and found the directions to his cabin sent in a text message to Henry.

I closed my eyes and tried to force the tears away.

Twenty minutes later, I had cleaned up the mess in the kitchen and put the extra food in the fridge. I didn't have any belongings other than the clothes I'd been wearing the day Blake found me. I also didn't have time to wash everything I'd been borrowing, so I left a note thanking Blake for his generosity and tossed everything into the washing machine.

It felt weird to wear the same thing Henry had seen me in when I fled from the cabin. It was even more embarrassing that I was wearing another pair of knee-high boots that had a broken heel—just like the ones his mother judged me for the first day we'd arrived.

Blake had been outside with Luna, avoiding me while I waited for Henry and his parents to arrive. The tension between us was so uncomfortable that I didn't blame him, though I also hated ending things this way.

I was pacing by the window, ignoring the beautifully decorated Christmas tree I had picked out and Blake had chopped down, when I saw a black Ford truck pull up in front of the cabin. I swallowed my nerves and my pride and walked outside. Blake was nowhere to be found, which might've been better since I wasn't sure I could handle saying goodbye to him.

Fifteen
Blake

Luna whimpered as the truck drove away, knowing that Holly was with them. She was gone, and I wasn't even man enough to say goodbye.

But honestly, I didn't trust myself not to get down on my knees and beg her to stay. Holly did something to me that I didn't understand. It was like she put a spell on me and had me willing to do anything and everything she asked just to see her happy.

Now she was on her way back to LA with her dumb-ass ex-boyfriend, who didn't deserve her, and his parents, who were probably judging her for breathing too loud in the backseat.

I took Luna inside, having had enough of the bitter cold. Even though the sun was shining, it was still hovering in the negative digits, and nothing was going to thaw this frozen heart of mine.

I tossed a few logs into the fire and headed to the laundry room to start a load since I'd been slacking on chores the past few days with Holly here. I set the hamper down and went to open the washer when I found a note on top.

Blake,

Thanks for saving me, in more ways than one.

XoXo

Holly

I held the paper in my hands and stared at it, wondering what in the world had changed her mind so quickly. I felt like things were going fine between us until she got the call from Henry, but maybe I was wrong. Maybe I just wanted to think that things were good between us because I was tired of being lonely.

In the end, it didn't matter. Holly chose to leave. She chose to go with Henry. I couldn't have changed any of that if I had tried.

I tossed the note in the trash and started the laundry.

By midday, I was going crazy being cooped up in the house. Every little thing reminded me of Holly, and I couldn't get her off my mind. There wasn't a safe space in the cabin that was free of thoughts of Holly.

Finally, I gave in and headed into town, knowing the roads were already cleared.

Shopping proved to be just as difficult as staying home when everything I saw made me think of her. From the plush bathrobe, I could picture her wearing after soaking for hours in my tub to the cute hoodie that would look adorable on her, it all pulled on my heartstrings so much that I found myself adding stuff to the cart that I had no intention of buying.

But apparently, I had taken crazy pills today because not

only did I buy stuff for Holly, but I also grabbed wrapping paper and tape so I could have gifts under the tree for someone who wouldn't be there to open them. I also picked up a few things for Luna and a bottle of whiskey for me since this was turning into the most depressing, pathetic Christmas I'd ever had in my life.

When I returned home, I was disappointed that Holly wasn't there. It wasn't like she was going to turn around and come running back to me—even though I desperately wanted her to.

Unfortunately, life just didn't work out that way.

<u>Sixteen</u>
Holly

I pretended to sleep the entire drive back to LA, which was longer than the drive to Hope Valley.

Henry tried to apologize when he got out of the truck to help me in, but I brushed him off and climbed inside without saying a word to his parents. I didn't owe them any pleasantries and was only taking Henry up on his offer for a ride back to LA because I had no other options that I could afford. In all fairness, this was the least he could do.

I had no idea what I was going to do once I got back to LA other than pack up my stuff and start looking for a new place. I had a few friends that I could reach out to, but it would only be temporary. I needed to figure out a plan for my life and didn't have any time to waste.

Once we got back, I went into the house without bothering to help Henry bring his stuff in. I knew that he would want to sit down and talk about things between us, but I didn't have the energy for it right now. I was drained—mentally, physically, and most of all—emotionally.

Leaving Blake felt harder than it should have, especially since I had only known him for a few days. But there was something about him that made me feel like I had known him my entire life. I was more comfortable around him than I had been with anyone else, even my own parents. He got me in a way no one ever had, which felt special. That was until he was ready to kick me out of his cabin and send me on my way.

I still had no idea what had happened and why there were so many mixed signals. He was a complicated man, but I thought I was finally starting to figure him out.

I heard Henry say goodbye to his parents and then closed the door. Needing my space from him, I brushed past him in the open foyer and headed toward the master bathroom.

"Holly, can we talk for a minute?"

"I'm going to soak."

I didn't wait for him to respond before I closed the door and locked it. I sat on the edge of the tub and let my fingers feel the trickle of water as I waited for it to get hot. Even though our house wasn't as big or as expensive as his parent's, I was going to miss this tub. It wasn't as fancy as the one at their cabin, but it was deep, and the water got the perfect temperature to soothe my achy body.

I added some bath salts and a squirt of my favorite bubble bath, then let it finish filling while I undressed and grabbed a clean towel from the linen closet.

As I passed the full-length mirror on the wall, I spotted the bruise on my hip and stopped.

It was big, just like Blake had said, but luckily it had started to fade. I trailed my fingers over it the same way he had. My eyes fluttered closed as I tried to remember his touch on my skin and the fire that had spread beneath.

My phone dinged with a new text message and snapped

me out of my trance. I dropped the towel to the floor by the tub and climbed in before checking it. Part of me hoped it was Blake, texting to make sure I got home okay, but then I remembered that he didn't have my number. Aside from directions to his cabin, I didn't have any other way to get in touch with him.

I responded to my friend and told him I could get my stuff moved over tomorrow since he was off and had a truck. I didn't want to spend Christmas here with Henry and didn't want to inconvenience anyone any more than I had to with it being so close to the holiday.

Disappointed with how things ended between Blake and me, I sank into the water and tried to wash my heartache away.

By the time I got out of the tub, my skin was wrinkly, and I felt somewhat better about things. That was until I walked down the hall and found Henry waiting for me on the couch.

"Holly, please," he said as he stood up and tried to stop me from walking past him. "I know that I messed up."

I yanked my arm out of his grip and glared at him.

"You think?"

"I'm sorry, Holly. Just tell me what to do, and I'll fix this."

"Fix what?" I asked with my hands on my hips.

"This—between us. Come on; we've been together for five years. We have a house together. We can't just walk away from that."

"You were literally just telling your dad about how you planned to break up with me and how you were interested in someone you work with. And now you want to *fix* this?

Henry, you didn't even bother to call and check on me after I left. You waited days and only called to ask about your car so you could get home."

He sighed and hung his head.

"The only thing that needs to be fixed is you, Henry. You're so concerned with what people think about you that you don't bother to figure out what you want for yourself. I'm not interested in being a part of that anymore. I know you want to try to make this work, but you can't fix what's been broken for so long. We got comfortable, and that's okay. But now that we know that neither of us is in love anymore, it's time to set each other free, so we can both be happy."

It felt good to say the words I'd been thinking in the tub out loud. I wasn't sure how I was going to handle things with Henry, but I trusted that I would figure it out when the time was right. Apparently, now was the time.

"I'm going to stay with Isaac for a while. He's helping me move tomorrow, but you don't have to be here."

He nodded and rubbed his lips together.

"I'll probably head into the office and give you some space."

"Thank you. I'll only take what's mine. You can keep anything we bought together."

"Holly, you don't have to do that."

"None of that matters to me. You know that. I'm a simple girl, Henry. I don't need money to make me happy."

It felt weird to say that because up until a few days ago, I was pretty sure that money did make me happy. But then I spent time with Blake and realized that it wasn't that at all.

I didn't need material things to be happy, I was just used to associating them with my happiness because Henry spent so much time trying to buy mine. Blake, on the other hand, gave me his time and attention, which was all I needed.

"Okay," he sighed. "But if you see something you want, you don't have to ask."

I nodded and headed down the other hall and to the guest room. It wasn't my house anymore, so I had no desire to sleep in the master bedroom with a man I barely knew anymore.

Seventeen
Holly

"What are we doing here?" I groaned as Isaac pulled me down another aisle, searching for the *perfect gift*. I had no clue who it was for, given that he had already finished all of his holiday shopping and it was already Christmas Eve.

"Shopping."

"For who?"

"Shhhh…."

He held up a finger and shook it at me, then pulled my hand and stopped in front of a cologne display. It was too early in the morning for this, and I definitely hadn't had enough coffee.

I tried to take a deep breath and calm the frustration that was building inside, but all I really wanted to do was go home—well, to Isaac's house, grab a pint of ice cream, a bottle of wine, a fluffy blanket, and crawl into bed.

My depression was in full swing, and I was the least jolly person around. But seriously, what was I supposed to be happy about? Tomorrow was Christmas, and I was single, homeless, and officially unemployed. I had absolutely nothing to look forward to.

Isaac talked with the woman who sprayed some of the cologne onto a small piece of paper, then waved it in the air and handed it to him. They talked about the scent and how it had hints of this and that, but I got bored and wandered off.

He was dating a new guy and wanted to impress his parents—even though I told him not to get his hopes up too high—which meant we were on the hunt for more gifts for him to shower them with when he met them for the first time on Christmas day. Talk about a lot of pressure.

I strolled down one of the aisles and stood in front of an artificial tree that had a few ornaments left hanging on it. I was about to walk off when I noticed that it looked almost identical to the one Blake had cut down for me. It was just about the same size and color, but this one had specks of white that were supposed to look like snow.

It was uncanny how much this one resembled his. I was about to blow it off and chalk it up to my constantly imagining things when my eyes landed on an ornament in the center of the tree.

I gasped and reached up, gently lifting the angel to my fingers.

A tear slid down my cheek as I continued to stare at it. While it couldn't possibly be the same one that Blake's mom had, it looked almost identical.

When Isaac approached, I was still lost in the moment, holding it in my hands.

"Whatcha got there?"

I looked up at him, my eyes red and tear-stained cheeks.

"What's wrong?"

I took a deep, shuddered breath and told him the story about Blake's mom and the angel she had been given.

"Wow. And it looks just like this one?"

I nodded.

"Well then, it's a sign."

"What is?" I asked, wiping my nose with a tissue as I sniffled.

"That you need to buy it for Blake."

"What?" I asked, pulling my head back in confusion.

"You said his mom thought the other angel was magical and brought people where they needed to be, right?"

"Yeah."

"So then this is your sign that you're meant to be with Blake. You found the only angel ornament in the damn store, which just happens to be hanging on a tree that looks like the one he cut down for you—it's a sign, Holly! This angel is taking you to where you belong."

I shook my head. There was no way he was right. These were just random coincidences.

"I know you don't believe in signs," he continued, nudging me with his elbow. "But if you don't trust that one, what about another one?"

I followed his finger as he pointed across the store where there was a display of custom engraved signs. At the top was one that read *Blake* with two angels beside the name.

No. Freaking. Way.

"Are you doing this?" I demanded, spinning to face him.

His cheeks split into a grin, showing off the dimples I loved.

My stomach fluttered at the thought of fate bringing Blake and me together again.

"So what do I do?"

"Listen and follow your heart. What does your heart want, Holly?"

I felt the corners of my lips turn up. I knew exactly what to do.

Eighteen
Blake

I had dozed off when Luna startled me awake with her barking. I jumped off the couch and spotted a beat-up truck pulling up out front beside mine. Not expecting any visitors, I watched from the window, waiting to see who it was before deciding what action to take.

The passenger door opened, and then Holly appeared. My heart stopped for a second as I blinked quickly, making sure I wasn't dreaming she was there.

When she nervously started heading toward the door, I rushed over and opened it for her.

"Holly, what are you doing here?"

She chewed her lip nervously and then looked over her shoulder. I couldn't tell who was in the truck with her, but I really hoped it wasn't Henry. I'd hate to have to kick his ass on Christmas Eve.

"I was at the store with my friend, Isaac," she said, pointing over her shoulder to the guy who had just gotten out. "And there was this artificial tree on display that looked just like the one we cut down. It made me think of you."

I leaned against the doorframe with my arms folded while Luna stayed at my side. Holly smiled at her and then looked back up at me.

"There weren't many ornaments on the tree, only a few that hadn't been purchased yet. But then this one seemed to appear magically and was hung in the middle, right where I could see it."

She walked closer and pulled something out of her pocket. Once she was in front of me, she pulled back the tissue paper and handed me the ornament.

My eyes widened as I studied it, noticing how it looked exactly like the one my mom had.

"I know this is a far stretch, Blake, and I'm sorry for just showing up uninvited. But I couldn't ignore the signs that I needed to come see you. I mean, they were everywhere. Like literally *everywhere*."

I rubbed my lips together, still staring at the ornament. I wasn't trying to make Holly feel uncomfortable, but I couldn't get my words out. My throat burned from the emotions that were bubbling up inside.

"I'm sorry, I should go. You can keep the ornament if you'd like. Or don't, it doesn't matter."

She turned and started to walk away when I began speaking.

"My mom thought the angel brought her where she needed to be in life. I think she was right, and now it's brought you to where you need to be."

She stopped and froze where she was.

"I don't know what's going on with you and Henry, but I know my life has been miserable without you, Holly. You deserve so much better. I know I'm not perfect, and I don't have much to offer, but if you give me a chance, I will love you like you need to be loved. I'll cherish and worship you every damn day. I'll—"

"There's no Henry," she interrupted, turning to face me.

"It's over?"

She nodded.

It felt almost too good to be true, but I didn't want to waste another second without having her in my arms. I nodded to her friend, who was grinning from ear to ear as I walked over and pulled her into my arms. She quickly wrapped her arms around my neck and pressed her lips to mine.

"You're the best gift I've ever gotten," I growled as I lifted her to my hips. She wrapped her legs around me and giggled before I captured it with a kiss.

"Does that mean you don't want the ones I bought you?" she giggled once she had her mouth free again.

I chuckled, knowing my mom must have had a hand in this all along. She showed Holly the angel and got me to purchase all of the stuff I got for Holly when I thought I'd never see her again.

After chatting for a few minutes with her friend, Isaac, we said goodbye and then went inside, where it was warm. I was thankful for him bringing Holly up to see me, even if he insisted that it was on his way and not a big deal. It was a huge deal to me.

I was more excited than a kid on Christmas morning, unable to believe I was spending the holiday with Holly.

This time she planned ahead and brought a small suitcase with her. At first, I thought it was just for an overnight stay and felt disappointed that our time was once again limited. But then she sadly admitted that she didn't take much when she moved out of Henry's house, and that was all she had in general. They had packed up her stuff from the cabin, but she said that when she sat down and looked through everything, she realized that all of the materialistic things didn't matter to her anymore. Plus, she left most of it with Henry as it was stuff he'd boughten her and she didn't want anymore reminders of him.

The thought of Holly officially moving in with me was mind-blowing in the best way possible.

We got her stuff situated, and I made a note to take her into town after Christmas to get the things she needed. I wanted her to feel at home here and not have everything be mine. Even though she only had a small suitcase full of personal belongings, she came with armfuls of gift bags that Isaac helped bring in before he left.

It turned out that they had been shopping this morning, and she decided on a whim to come up here when she found out Isaac was already headed this way to go to his boyfriend's parent's house for Christmas. She sat in the backseat of his truck and wrapped gifts on the drive out here. Thankfully the roads were all cleared so they didn't have too many delays, other than heavy traffic here and there.

I offered to cook dinner, but Holly insisted that we eat a bowl of cereal and call it a night since it was so late. Once I saw her in the new pajamas that she'd bought for tonight, I didn't object one little bit.

Nineteen
Holly

"Is that a candy cane in your stocking, or are you just happy to see me?" I teased, rubbing my butt against the morning wood that was greeting me.

It felt good to wake up in Blake's bed again, but even better to be wrapped in his arms.

"What can I say? Santa has packages to deliver." He nipped my ear and then licked his way down my neck to my shoulder. "Have you been a good girl?"

I moaned as he reached forward and caressed my breast before moving his hand down to my pussy and teasing my lips.

"Nope."

He rolled me off my side onto my back.

"Do you know what Santa does to naughty girls?"

I pulled my bottom lip between my teeth and shook my head.

His eyes danced with excitement as his fingers trailed over my pussy, finally pushing one inside.

"He makes them come."

"Is that so?" I breathed out, closing my eyes as he inserted another finger.

"It is. And he spanks them."

"Mmmmm…."

He pumped his fingers faster, spreading my wetness between my folds.

I was close already, which was quite surprising given how many times I came last night. I didn't know my body was capable of having that many orgasms in such a short time.

Just as I was starting to get close, he pulled out and licked his lips.

"Ready for your punishment, naughty girl?"

I grinned; the damp fabric between my thighs confirmed that I was.

He rolled me over and lifted my waist to get me onto my knees. I loved this position and he knew it.

I spread my legs and lifted my ass, waiting for him to roll a condom on his hard cock. Then I felt the bed dip as he climbed up and spanked my ass, sending a jolt of pleasure and pain through me at once.

"Ahh," I cried out as he did it again. Before I could adjust to the sting of it, he slid inside and began thrusting.

I moved my neck, allowing him to kiss me while I frantically rubbed my clit, desperate for the orgasm that was building so quickly.

A few minutes later, I felt him grab my wrist and stop my hand.

"I make you come," he growled and replaced my fingers with his.

I whimpered as he kept the rhythm and brought me to climax within seconds while he continued to thrust hard before coming in the condom.

"Best. Christmas. Ever." I sighed contentedly and fell onto the pillows after he pulled out.

Once we were both cleaned up and dressed, we went to the living room and sat down on the floor in front of the tree. We'd added my gifts to the pile when I got there yesterday, but I was still shocked that he'd taken the time and energy to buy me gifts when he didn't even know that he would see me again.

He handed me a box wrapped with a gold bow, and I gave him a gift bag that had several wrapped gifts inside. Luna was already busy chewing the bone I got her last night and couldn't be bothered with our festivities.

I opened mine first and pulled out a light pink hoodie and matching leggings, both fleece lined and super warm. I grinned stupidly as I thought about how I would be comfortable here without having to steal any more of his clothes—even though I was still going to just because I liked how he looked at me when I was wearing them.

He opened his gift and smiled when he held up the wooden sign I'd convinced them to sell me from the display. The owner was reluctant until I told him my story, and his wife made him give it to me. It was perfect with his name and the two angels on it—the one his mom originally had and the one we believe she helped me find.

We continued opening gifts, and I was amazed at how thoughtful he was in his gifts for me. Besides warm clothes and bath products, he'd also grabbed me some snacks that he knew I liked, which was going to make today that much more special.

I'd grabbed a few sentimental things for him and then let Isaac shop for some of the other stuff. He was impressed with the insulated gloves Isaac insisted he needed and the new pocketknife. It was fun shopping for each other, but I could only imagine how great it would be once we knew each other better. This was such a whirlwind start, but I wouldn't change a single thing about it.

"So, what did you want to do today?" he asked as I laid against his chest on the couch.

We hadn't bothered to clean up the mess from opening gifts, and I was in no rush to. It felt good to just be with him.

"I didn't have any plans. Maybe watch movies? Play a board game? You?"

"Nothing either. But we're probably stuck inside for a few days. There's another bad storm moving in tonight."

I looked outside and noticed the white clouds hovering above the trees. It seemed like getting snowed in together was our thing now, and I had no problem with it. Memories of making love to him to pass the time flooded through me and spread heat throughout my body.

"Don't worry," I assured. "I know some things we can do inside."

His fingers tickled my sides as I felt him hardening beneath me. It was going to be a good Christmas, indeed.

****

Ready for more steamy Christmas romance? Be sure to check out these other novellas!

Snow Place To Go https://books2read.com/u/4A560N

A Christmas Wish https://books2read.com/u/4EKXpE

Blame It On The Mistletoe https://books2read.com/u/bw1rqe

Blame It On The Eggnog https://books2read.com/u/38PPY6

<u>Other Books By Samantha Baca</u>

<u>The Haven Brook Series</u>
<u>(small-town romantic suspense):</u>

'Til Death Do Us Part (Haven Brook Book 1)

https://books2read.com/u/m2RJNR

The Cradle Will Fall (Haven Brook Book 2)

https://books2read.com/u/b6O0QE

The Ties That Bind (Haven Brook Book 3)

https://books2read.com/u/mqgoz8

A Very Haven Christmas (Haven Brook Book 4- Novella)

https://books2read.com/u/mvqGjj

Three Strikes, You're Gone (Haven Brook Book 5)

https://books2read.com/u/mvqL2z

The Dark Shadows Series (romantic suspense)

Five Steps Ahead (Dark Shadows Book 1)

https://books2read.com/u/38Q0gO

Ten Seconds Too Late (Dark Shadows Book 2)

https://books2read.com/u/3JRgVB

Against The Clock (Dark Shadows Book 3)

https://books2read.com/u/m2YwoR

Out Of Time (Dark Shadows Book 4)

https://books2read.com/u/4DKMoP

The Stone Creek Series (small-town- novellas)

Chocolate Covered Mistletoe (Stone Creek Book 1)

https://books2read.com/u/3LRk9N

Candy Coated Promises (Stone Creek Book 2)

https://books2read.com/u/mldP5Y

Pumpkin Spiced Possibilities (Stone Creek Book 3)

https://books2read.com/u/bojdwV

Beaumont Creek Series (small town)
Just One Time (Beaumont Creek Book 1)
https://books2read.com/u/3G52zK

Second Chances (Beaumont Creek Book 2)
https://books2read.com/u/4Aj6Z0

Third Time's The Charm (Beaumont Creek Book 3)
https://books2read.com/u/b5lEyG

Four-ever Single (Beaumont Creek Book 4)
Preorder link coming soon

Fifth Wheel (Beaumont Creek Book 5)
Preorder link coming soon

Whiskey Mountain Series (small-town- novellas)
Something To Talk About
https://books2read.com/u/4X62ag

Something To Think About
https://books2read.com/u/3GWAan

Something To Believe In
https://books2read.jjom/u/3yVzgB

Something To Live For
Preorder link coming soon

Sugarplum Falls Series
(Holiday Novellas- can be read as standalone)

Blame It On The Mistletoe

https://books2read.com/u/bw1rqe

Blame It On The Eggnog

https://books2read.com/u/38PPY6

Standalone Books

One Last Wish

https://books2read.com/u/mqg7D9

Finding Love In Apartment 2C (novella)

https://books2read.com/u/bze9aZ

Cocky Counsel: A Hero Club Novel

https://books2read.com/u/31Kzkn

All Is Fair In Food And War (novella)

https://books2read.com/u/bp8qjX

Holiday Books (novellas)

Snow Place To Go

https://books2read.com/u/4A560N

A Christmas Wish

https://books2read.com/u/4EKXpE

Holiday Hijinks

https://books2read.com/u/4DP6Ze

<u>Acknowledgments</u>

As always, I'd like to start by thanking all of the wonderful readers who picked up my book and decided to read it! Thank you! I really hope you enjoyed this fun, steamy, holiday romance. Even though it was short, I hope it gave you a chance to escape for a little bit and provided a few laughs.

I'm so thankful to my alpha and beta readers. You guys have been there for me through twenty books and I can't imagine working through another one without you. Thank you so much!

I wouldn't be where I am in life without the love and support of my family. That goes for everything with my books too. Thank you for always being there and cheering me on!

My girls are the light of my life and bring so much happiness to my world. I hope that someday you both chase after your dreams the way that I've gone after mine. I can't wait to see what you do my loves.

Richard, I love you and your constant support of me and my books—even if you remind me how dirty I am. I couldn't imagine a better partner to embark on all of these journeys with and I am so thankful to have you by my side.

Thank you again for reading this novella! If you've enjoyed it and wouldn't mind leaving an honest review on your favorite platform, I would greatly appreciate it!

About the Author

Samantha lives in the southwest with her husband and two small children after abandoning her childhood dream of living in a cabin in Colorado when she found that she couldn't afford to live there and was deathly allergic to the woods. When she's not writing, she's usually spouting off sarcastic remarks while drinking wine out of a coffee mug to look like a functional adult while chasing down her toddlers. She enjoys spending time with her family, watching reruns of Friends, and the 24/7 flow of coffee that can be found in her veins. Be sure to follow her on social media for updates on what she's working on.

You can find her here:

Facebook: https://www.facebook.com/AuthorSamanthaBaca

Instagram: https://instagram.com/author_samantha_baca

Goodreads: http://www.goodreads.com/authorsamanthabaca

Facebook Reader Group: https://www.facebook.com/groups/2945710968775398/

Webpage: https://authorsamanthabaca.wordpress.com

Newsletter: http://eepurl.com/g0NcSj